FRIENDS FIRST ✍ **W9-BZO-544**

Miranda and Gus have been best friends since they were little kids. She's closer to him than any girl she knows—and now all of the girls she knows think he's her boyfriend. That's one of the things that happens in eighth grade, just like a busier school schedule and boy–girl dances. Miranda expected it—but she didn't expect to feel so alone. First Emma, who's practically her second mother, quits her job as the family housekeeper. Then, one horrible night near Christmas, a strange man attacks Miranda in her apartment building. No one is there to help, and when Gus tries to console her afterwards, she finds it hard to trust him—or any man. Growing up is hard enough. Why does it have to be so much harder for girls?

"A brave statement, particularly as occasioned in the junior-high genre."
—*Bulletin of the Center for Children's Books*

"Insightfully explores mature subject matter with clarity and sensitivity." —*Children's Book Review Service*

"[Miranda's] exploration of the nature of friendship and the problems of maturing make pleasant light reading." —*Kirkus Reviews*

ALSO BY CHRISTINE MCDONNELL

Don't Be Mad, Ivy

Toad Food and Measle Soup

Lucky Charms and Birthday Wishes

Just for the Summer

Count Me In

Friends First

CHRISTINE McDONNELL

PUFFIN BOOKS

For my students, with love. You inspire me.

PUFFIN BOOKS
Published by the Penguin Group
Penguin Books USA Inc., 375 Hudson Street, New York, New York 10014, U.S.A.
Penguin Books Ltd, 27 Wrights Lane, London W8 5TZ, England
Penguin Books Australia Ltd, Ringwood, Victoria, Australia
Penguin Books Canada Ltd, 10 Alcorn Avenue, Toronto, Ontario, Canada M4V 3B2
Penguin Books (N.Z.) Ltd, 182–190 Wairau Road, Auckland 10, New Zealand

Penguin Books Ltd, Registered Offices: Harmondsworth, Middlesex, England

First published in the United States of America by Viking Penguin,
a division of Penguin Books USA Inc., 1990
Published in Puffin Books, 1992

1   3   5   7   9   10   8   6   4   2

LIBRARY OF CONGRESS CATALOGING-IN-PUBLICATION DATA
McDonnell, Christine.
Friends first / by Christine McDonnell.   p.   cm.
Summary: An eighth grade girl faces the evolving relationships,
complex changes, and changing feelings arising from her
first steps into adulthood.
ISBN 0-14-032477-1
I. Title.
[PZ7.M47843Fr 1992]   [Fic]—dc20   92-20290

Printed in the United States of America
Set in Sabon

1

"What a way to end the summer—rained out," Gus said. He balanced his two-foot model rocket across his knees and traced the smooth edges of the fins, and the nose cone's narrow red-and-black stripes.

"The rain might stop," I said, knowing how disappointed he was. He'd been working on the model for two weeks, and he'd just finished mounting a new ignition switch inside a cigar box.

"No way, Space Central says the launch is postponed until Saturday due to unsettled atmospheric conditions."

"And school starting," I said.

"Right. Unsettled atmospheric conditions and school."

We were sitting on Gus's window seat in the attic of our house. When Sebastian, Gus's little brother, was born five years ago, his father made a room for Gus in half the attic. He built a bed along one wall, opened a skylight above it for stargazing, put up shelves for Gus's books and rockets, and across the front, under the triple window at the peak of the house, he built a window seat. Gus read there, and wrote in his notebooks, and I often sat there with him, looking out through the trees at the clutter of Boston roofs, chimneys, and steeples.

Rain slithered down the glass. "Race you," I said, pointing to the raindrops. It was an old game of ours. We bet on raindrops rolling down the window at the same time. First drop to reach the sill won. Gus always picked fat ones. "Extra weight pulls them down," he said. "Law of gravity." Sometimes the little fast drops won anyway.

"I give up," I said after Gus's fatties won five in a row, and went downstairs to my apartment to get a book to read. Gus went to get us iced tea.

Gus Llewellyn was my first friend. He'd always lived upstairs from me. When we were babies our mothers wheeled our strollers down to the playground every day. I bet they talked about the exciting stuff they did before staying home with us. Gus and I probably ate sand and pushed each other over learning to walk.

I came back upstairs and crossed through the Llewellyns' living room with my book. In the kitchen, Gus was wheedling cookies from his mother. "Half a box, just half. Come on, Mom, they're Lorna Doones." The hall outside the kitchen was covered with family photographs and pictures of Gus's soccer teams. Both our families have a million photos of Gus and me together as babies. First children get photographed. Poor Sebastian, there aren't half as many of him. I was bald, mostly. Mom says I had a layer of fine blond fuzz, but in pictures I look bald, with a head shaped like Tweetie Bird's. Gus, sitting beside me on couches, wagons, steps, and swings, is curly-topped. He smiled for the camera, but I usually stared blankly or glared at it with a questioning look. I wonder what I was thinking about. Smiling Gus and Solemn Miranda.

"Augustus, will you stop! You could beg millions from a miser. I am so glad this summer's over. You wear me out!"

"You'll miss me, Mom. I make your life exciting."

"Ha! This is exciting? Keeping your cookie habit satisfied? Shoveling dirty towels off the bathroom floor? No, Gus, winning the lottery is exciting. A weekend in London without kids is exciting. For parents, school vacation is *not* exciting. Here, take the box and give me peace."

Gus grabbed it and kissed her cheek. "You'll miss me tomorrow, Mom. I know you will."

Gus's mother, Carol, is my mother's best friend. They were just neighbors at first: Carol and Matt, Gus's father, lived in the upstairs apartment, and my parents lived downstairs. But after Gus and I were born, Mom and Carol got to know each other. They became especially close the year Gus and I turned two, when my father died in a car accident, sideswiped by a drunk driver on the expressway. He had his seat belt on but it didn't help. Matt and Carol helped Mom get through that year. Mom says she spent hours at their kitchen table drinking raspberry tea with Carol and listening to Beatles records and the Modern Jazz Quartet. They planned imaginary trips to Greece, China, and Nepal. She and Carol took a yoga course together while Matt baby-sat for us. Mom says she couldn't have made it without the Llewellyns.

A year after the accident, when I was three, Mom went to law school using the insurance money, and Emma Bounty, our housekeeper, moved in with us and took care of me. When Emma had an evening off and Mom had a class or a lot of work, I'd head upstairs with my pajamas, toothbrush, and my stuffed dog, Mr. Bones. The Llewellyns became my second family and Gus became my best friend.

We settled back on the window seat again, one of us at each end. Gus sat with his grasshopper legs folded, otherwise his feet would reach all the way to my side. "Have a cookie," he said. We each took four. He opened his notebook and began to write. As usual, he was working on a science fiction story. I opened my book, a teenage romance.

Since sixth grade, I'd read so many teenage romance books that they blurred together in my mind. The main character is always a girl who wants a boyfriend. She sails or trains dogs or rides horses or works in a hospital. She's not dumb or ugly, but nobody has noticed her yet because she wears braces or glasses or she needs a new haircut or different clothes or she's too shy or new in town. All the books take place in a town: in Vermont near a ski slope; on a Maine island; in Hawaii or California or Colorado or Wyoming. Some little town with window boxes where people talk to each other at the grocery store and the post office. The girls' names always end in *y, i,* or *ie:* Cindi, Mindy, Stacy, Tracy, Trixie, Pixie, etc.

I didn't believe the stories in these books. I know life isn't like a teenage romance novel. Once, though, when I was ten, I did think of changing my name to Trixie. I thought that in high school, when I started dating and some boy went to whisper in my ear, Trixie would sound better than Miranda. But now I think Trixie sounds like a poodle and I know boys don't whisper in your ear, anyway.

Gus was writing and I was reading and chewing on my hair. It's a bad habit, I admit, but it doesn't show as much as biting your nails.

"Did Cindi meet the lifeguard yet?"

"He's not a lifeguard in this one. I finished *Hawaiian Sunset.* This one's in Vermont. He's on the ski patrol and her name is Marci." I poked him with my toe. "It's no worse than science fiction."

Gus was staring out the window with the squinched-up look he gets when he's starting a new plan. "We should write a science fiction romance. *Tracy Meets the Alien. Extraterrestial at the Prom.* Wait, I've got a good one. *Alien Attraction.* You write the description of the girl and I'll write the alien. Then we'll put them together."

I closed my book. The only way to avoid being in one

5

of Gus's schemes was to leave, and I was comfortable on the window seat. Gus gave me one of his special notebooks with the light green paper.

"We have to decide where this takes place," I said.

"Alaska. Put everybody in parkas with fur around the hoods. Stick in dogsleds, huskies, polar bears."

"Maybe we should figure out the plot first," I stalled.

"My mother says the story comes from the characters. She says it all the time, especially when she's stuck. Just start describing the girl. Say anything you want. You can always change it."

I started. I gave her red hair. I liked red hair, especially that very curly, bushy red hair. People who have that hair usually hate it and complain about it. I tried to think of a name to go along with red hair. It had to have the right ending. Patsy. Pookie. Terry. Terry with the bushy red curls. What did she do in Alaska? She had a pet seal pup. No, that was dumb.

"I don't want this to be in Alaska. Let's put it right here."

Gus agreed. "But if it gets boring, we'll move it to the alien's planet."

"Miranda, Emma's calling you," Carol yelled up the stairs.

I clipped the pen onto the front cover of the notebook.

"What's her name?" Gus asked.

"Who?"

"The girl in the story."

"Terry. Short for Teresa."

6

"Teresa's a nice name. Tell Teresa that Vortrum says good-bye."

"Vortrum?"

"The alien. Vortrum. From Interstixus, Galaxy Urna, beyond the Sea of Fire. Vortrum, Rocket Patrol Training Cadet. But he'd rather be home growing astroplants."

I could hear Emma two floors down.

"Good-bye, Vortrum."

2

Waking up early for school was a shock. I slouched into the kitchen still groggy. My uniform jumper itched, the required knee socks made my feet sweat, and the blouse kept bunching up around my waist. Emma ignored my gloom and kissed me on the cheek. Then, humming "Oh, What a Beautiful Morning," she pushed my hair back off my forehead and straightened my collar. I shoved her hands away before she could button my top button.

"Emma, *stop!* I'm not a baby. You don't have to dress me. And I like my hair the way it is."

I shook it down over my face and tossed it loosely back.

It was straight and came down to just below my shoulders. I liked it casual. I wished it had blond streaks but it was all plain light brown. Emma still optimistically bought me plastic headbands, three to a pack—pink, blue, and white. I hadn't worn a headband since fourth grade.

"The Good Lord gave you a lovely forehead, you should show it," Emma said. "And don't frown like that, Miranda, someday your face might freeze. Come and have breakfast."

I flopped into a chair and sank my head down on the table. "I'm not hungry, Emma. I just want to sleep."

"You can get to bed early tonight. I won't have you heading to school with an empty stomach. The bus'll be here in fifteen minutes."

"The van," I said.

"Bus, van, what's the difference?" Emma laughed. "It's coming, whatever you call it."

They called it a bus but it was a van with M.A.A. written on the side, for Miss Ayers Academy. Back in kindergarten, the first time I rode the school bus, I waited on the front steps, with my new uniform on and my hair in braids, blue ribbons on the ends to match the navy jumper. I thought the jumper was beautiful. I even liked the lower-school oxfords. Everything was shiny and crisp, with a new smell like spray starch. I hoped that everyone on the block would see me and know that Miranda Boyd was old enough to go to school.

Starting eighth grade was nothing like that. I hated the thought of seeing the same girls, sitting in the same white rooms with wood trim, looking at the same green boards and reproductions of famous paintings. The teachers stuck pictures everywhere to sneak more culture into us. Miss Ayers was strict, snobby, and old-fashioned. At Gus's school, they had gymnastics and took Spanish and World Cultures. At Miss Ayers, we played field hockey and studied Hygiene instead of Sex Education.

I finished my cereal and kissed Emma good-bye. I was still sulking about starting school, but I let her push my hair back again and I didn't shake it forward until I was outside. It wasn't her fault that I hated school.

While I sat on the front steps, Gus came out the door holding an English muffin in his teeth, with his soccer ball under his arm and his backpack over one shoulder. He walked to school, lucky him, since Bigelow Junior High was only eight blocks away. I wished my mother would let me go there, but she was fussy about school.

"Waiting for the bus?" He offered me a bite and sat down to wait with me.

I put my foot next to his, measuring the difference. My uniform loafers were hard and shiny, without the creases that come with breaking in. They could be anybody's shoes. Next to them, Gus's long green hightops with colored-marker doodles were unmistakably his. If you put our shoes in the middle of a pile at a birthday party game, Gus would have no trouble and I wouldn't have a chance.

"I wish I could wear sneakers to school," I said.

Gus nodded. "School's bad enough without a uniform," he said. "Want me to scuff those up for you?" He scraped his sneaker soles across the fronts of my loafers, streaking the shine. "That's better," he said. He opened his backpack and pulled out a rocket catalogue. "Look what I'm going to send for next. It's a multistage rocket with a passenger compartment. You can send up mice, or bugs. If your hamster was still alive, we could send her up."

I poked in the backpack, curious about what else Gus was bringing to school. There was a neon green Frisbee, a red-and-black Hacky Sack, two Dungeons and Dragons books, and a peanut butter sandwich, dry. Gus said jelly diluted the taste. Peanut butter plain was all Carol could get him to eat for lunch. Never turkey or ham or tuna. Just PB on white bread cut in triangles with the crusts trimmed off.

"Here comes the bus, good old M. A. A.," Gus said. "*Maa. Maa*," he bleated, like a dumb sheep. It was an old joke between us. He walked me to the curb. "Maybe there'll be somebody new in your class, somebody you like," he said, trying to cheer me up.

I nodded and climbed in, waving good-bye when I got a seat. The bus paused halfway up the block while a car backed into a parking space, and I watched Gus amble by, tossing and catching his soccer ball. He was whistling. He always whistled. His long legs glided out in front of him. His hair was as curly as Harpo's, but short. He had a little smile on his face as he whistled.

"Is that your boyfriend?" Morna Hollister turned around in the seat in front of me to ask.

"He's my friend. He lives upstairs from me."

"He's cute. What grade's he in?"

"Eighth, same as us."

"He looks older. Is he on a soccer team?"

I shrugged, wanting to end the conversation. If Morna got ideas about Gus, she'd hound me to invite her over so she could meet him. Then I'd have to watch her blink at him and laugh this dumb little giggle that she uses when boys are around. She sounds deranged.

At school we said, "Hi," and "Had a great summer," even if it wasn't true. I found Louise and Millie, my friends from seventh grade, and we wandered around looking for our lockers and study hall desks. My old best friend at school, Eleanor, had moved to New York in August.

My new study hall desk was next to the window so I could look out at the ginkgo tree and the lower-school playground. Back a few years, in third or fourth grade, a teacher told us that the ginkgo lost all its leaves on the same day. I always wanted to see that but every year I missed it. One day, the tree would be covered in yellow leaves. The next day, the leaves would be lying thick on the ground. Maybe this year I'd see them fall.

Inside my desk I found a pile of books: a brown assignment book with my name, *M. Boyd*, in italic letters on the front; a word list for eighth-grade vocabulary and spelling; a grammar book, just as boring as last year's; a poetry folder; a math book; a science book; an atlas; a history book with a picture of the Lincoln Memorial on the front, and a reading anthology called *Journeys*—at least that looked interesting.

Next to me a skinny sixth grader, up from the lower school for the first time, was sharpening her pencils with a pencil sharpener shaped like a miniature globe of the world. When she lifted the lid of her desk I saw a stuffed tiger hidden in the back corner. I introduced myself, knowing she'd be too shy to go first.

"I'm Danielle," she answered. "Where do we go now?" She looked as if she might cry—her eyes were shiny and her lip quivered.

"Probably to the assembly hall for the opening talk. Then back here and then to your first class. Just follow me and relax. It's not that different from lower school."

"Oh, yes, it is," she said. She lifted her desk lid again, and, pretending to rearrange her books, she stroked her tiger.

Standing in front, with the green velvet curtains behind her and the school motto, "Ladies and Leaders," carved in the arch above the stage, Miss Campion, the headmistress, gave the usual opening day speech about Evangeline Ayers, who founded the school for the proper education of young women of breeding. Sounded like horses to me. Then she listed a lot of rules, nothing new. When Miss Campion talked, she only moved her lower lip and chin, never the top half of her face. I asked my mother if she'd had a stroke, or was paralyzed so that her face couldn't move. "No, she does that deliberately. Some people think it's elegant," Mom said. I thought she looked like a cheap cartoon where only the mouth moves in the middle of the face.

That first day back, the only surprise came in English class. Miss Jerome, last year's eighth grade teacher, had gotten married over the summer and moved to Chicago. When we walked into class after assembly, Miss Rathbone was standing in the corner, leaning against the board, gazing out the window. I didn't see her at first, since I expected the teacher to be in the front of the room. Everyone was shoving to get to the seat they wanted, next to their best friend, and squealing, "Sit here, sit here." I was aiming for the window seat in the last row, that's how I noticed her.

She smiled at me and said softly, "Why not move up front?"

She sounded so conversational that I answered honestly, "I like the window."

"So do I," she said.

So I stayed in the back row, next to the windowsill. A new girl took the seat beside me, another back row person. Miss Rathbone didn't say a word about the noise. She stood very still watching the class until they quieted down. Then she walked to the center of the room. She had a rounded back and orthopedic shoes, and I expected her to shuffle, but her step had a bounce. She scanned the class silently, looking from face to face. I wanted to look down at my desk but her gaze forced me to meet her eyes. When she finally spoke, her voice was low and calm.

"Good morning, girls. Most of you know me. This year, I will be teaching you English and History."

We knew her by sight and reputation. She was Director of Studies for the whole school, and she'd always taught the senior class. Everyone said she was the smartest teacher in the school, and also the hardest.

"Perhaps you wonder why I have decided to teach your grade. It interests me, that's why."

That's all she said about it that day.

At recess, I watched the cliques herd together. The worst was Cynthia Havelock's group. She was the queen, and she had four clones. I called them Cynthia One, Cynthia Two, Cynthia Three, etc. This year the Cynthias had two earrings in each ear, one tiny stud and a long dangler, and they wore their hair pulled to one side in ponytails. They each wore four bangle bracelets on the left arm, and little silver rings, at least three on each hand. Oh, yes, and their eyes. They wore pinky-purple eyeliner. It was spooky to see them, all exactly alike like that. It made the rest of us look distinctive, even in our uniforms.

Cynthia One sat at the top of the gym stairs with the other Cynthias below her on the steps. She commented on everyone else in the class and the others echoed her verdict. "She doesn't need a bra." "Needs to pluck her eyebrows." "Guys don't like girls that tall."

I stood across the courtyard, leaning on a tree, watching. I didn't see the new girl until she spoke to me.

"Don't you hate being stuck inside when it's like this out?" She pointed to the sky. "If I didn't have to be here, I'd ride my bike as far up the river as I could go. Or I'd play tennis all day." She smiled. Her teeth were buried under braces. "My name's Catherine. What did you think of Rathbone? I can't believe we're going to read Dickens.

Did you see how long that book was? Maybe she forgot we're just in eighth grade."

The bell rang for third period.

"Sit beside me in Math," I said.

She smiled and her braces sparkled.

"Tinsel Teeth. Watch out for the metal detector at the airport," I heard Cynthia say as we went up the steps.

I wanted to speak up right then, turn around and challenge her right to her face. But I didn't. I wasn't sure Catherine had heard her. I didn't want to make an enemy for her, or for me. Okay, I chickened out.

3

Every year in September, Mom and I climb Digby Mountain. It's a ritual, like going out to dinner on our birthdays, decorating the tree on Christmas Eve, and swimming at Hackett's Pond on Memorial Day unless there's rain.

"The weather report says cool and sunny. Let's climb on Saturday," Mom said.

We were sitting in the living room after dinner. I was describing my first day back at school—my new friend, Catherine, the Cynthias' pierced ears and bracelets, Rathbone reading the myth of Persephone. "Persephone was out picking flowers on an ordinary sunny day when Hades

17

came roaring out of the underworld in his black chariot and grabbed her. He took her prisoner, dragged her down to his kingdom, and made her sit beside him on the throne. She cried the whole time. What a bully."

"Did she escape?" Mom asked.

"Her mother, Demeter, saved her. She was Goddess of the Harvest and she kept spring from coming until she got Persephone back."

Mom nodded, satisfied. "Good old Mom. What will this be, our seventh climb?" she asked.

I counted on my fingers. "Eighth. We started the year I went into first grade."

"But one year we were rained out," Mom said.

"Fourth grade, but we climbed in the spring instead."

"And there weren't any blueberries."

"Daniel came with us," I said. He was Mom's boyfriend then. Since my father died, she had had three serious boyfriends: Bernie, Daniel, and Jim, one at a time in that order. Bernie made lasagna, Daniel had a beard, and Jim wore glasses and taught me how to play piano rags. I thought she'd marry Daniel because he spent so much time with us, but he moved to the country when I was in sixth grade. When we visited him, we climbed the hill behind his house and picked wildflowers. I made Mom a crown and Daniel made her a bracelet and a ring. On the way home, I asked Mom if she was going to marry him. She laughed and said how could she practice bankruptcy law in a hick town full of farmers and aging hippies.

When we climbed Digby, we always packed our lunch in plastic containers, then filled them with blueberries on the way down. Digby's bald head is dotted with blueberry bushes that grow in the hollows and the crevices of the rocks. In early September, there are plenty to pick. We bring the containers home and Emma makes muffins and blueberry pancakes.

Mom pulled into the parking area at the foot of the trail, climbed out of the car, and stretched. She hiked in shorts when it was warm enough. She spread mosquito repellant all over her arms and legs, still freckled from our week at the beach, and around her neck and the edge of her face. She was tall and thin, a pole like me, but her hair was dark and wavy, cut short. I got my hair and eyes from my father. I knew from the photograph album and the picture on the mantel of my father standing by his bike somewhere in Nova Scotia. The sun is shining on his hair and making him squint, but I know his eyes were gray and his hair was just like mine, light brown and straight.

We started up the logging road, the easy trail. The direct route was shorter, but the long trail gave us more time and breath to talk. Mom walked in front of me, her green backpack bouncing a little with each stride. The sun splattered through the trees. A few had begun to change color, but most were still green and full.

After half an hour of quiet walking, Mom stopped to pull off her jacket and tie a rolled bandanna around her forehead. She pulled out her water bottle, drank a few swallows, and handed it to me. The water was still cold. I took off my sweatshirt and stuffed it into my backpack. The bugs hadn't appeared yet.

Halfway up the trail a rock jutted out, forming a ledge

19

like an easy chair. We sat with our legs dangling and passed the water bottle back and forth. Mom peeled an orange and split it in half. Then she tilted her face to the sun and I looked down at the fields. A tractor moved slowly up and down the rows. It reminded me of the view from Daniel's hill.

"Why didn't you marry Daniel?" I asked.

She didn't open her eyes, but she smiled. "You liked him, didn't you?"

"Why do you say that?"

"You never ask why I didn't marry Jim or Bernie."

"Why didn't you?"

"Same reason that I didn't marry Daniel. I didn't want to." She opened her eyes and looked at me. "I did think about marrying Daniel. Maybe if he'd stayed in the city, I would have. It's hard to fit lives together."

"What about Jim?" Jim, the piano player, had been her most recent boyfriend. She dated him when I was in seventh grade, but stopped seeing him in the spring.

She yawned. "Jazzy Jim. Did you like him?"

I shrugged.

"After a while we had nothing to talk about," she said. "He hated to hear about law, said it could put anyone to sleep. He worked nights, I worked days." She blew out a long stream of air, making her lips vibrate. "The lawyer and the piano man. We didn't jive, as Jim would say."

A mosquito landed on my calf and I flattened him before he had a chance to bite. Mom handed me the insect repellant.

"Do you think I should get married?" she said.

I shrugged again.

"Maybe I should. I liked being married to your father. I don't know why I haven't married again." She shielded her eyes and looked down at the fields. "Daniel was a sweetheart, wasn't he? I wonder what he's up to. I bet he's found some lovely country lady and settled down." She stood up and put on her backpack. "Don't look back, or you'll turn into salt," she said.

I followed her off the ledge onto the trail. "Why salt?"

"Don't they teach you any Bible stories at Miss Ayers? When God destroyed Sodom and Gomorrah, he saved Lot and his wife. He let them escape but he told them not to look back. Lot's wife was too curious, or maybe she worried about her friends or the rest of her family. She looked back and was turned into a pillar of salt. So don't look back." She waved me forward up the trail. "At least not until we get to the top."

We reached the ledges after noon. After we ate lunch, Mom read for a while and I lay on my back and watched the clouds.

A cloud shaped like a hippo on its back reminded me of Gus. He liked very big animals—bears, elephants, whales, giant tortoises, rhinos—anything strong or enormous. Gus would have liked it on top of Digby, close to the sky. He loved space.

I shook the crumbs out of the lunch containers and started to hunt for blueberries. At first I could only find one or two on a branch. But when I moved down a little, off the north side, I could pull handfuls. I filled my two containers easily. Mom filled hers, too, and we started down.

As I watched her walk ahead of me, I thought about her question. I didn't care if she stayed single. She'd been single this long, what difference did it make? She didn't seem lonely. Why would she be lonely with me and Emma at home, and the Llewellyns upstairs? I liked the men she dated, but we didn't need them. I liked things just the way they were. Why change things when they're running smoothly?

4

At Miss Ayers, I'd been hearing about Hygiene class for years, in dozens of corny jokes. Hi, Jean. That skirt's too high, Jean. In eighth grade, I finally got the real thing. We had it in the upper school biology lab. I think the teacher hoped we'd take it more seriously if we met there. Some people complained that the school needed new facilities but I loved the old lab with its tall windows and hanging lamps. The walls were lined with shelves of jars, flasks, and welded metal apparatus—like a lab from the Theater of Thrills. The floor was slate and the lab tables and stools were dark wood. A dusty stuffed owl and a faded hawk sat on top of the back counter, next to a row of Bunsen burners. Behind them hung butterfly specimens mounted under glass, and bird and insect nests. Catherine and I grabbed seats at the back table, near the owl. Louise and Millie sat with us.

We had Hygiene before Rathbone's class on Tuesday and Thursday. The other three days we had Latin. I liked Latin better. If you learned the vocabulary and remembered the rules, you could actually read it. I liked the order of it, the predictability.

Our Hygiene teacher, Miss LeBlond, also coached field hockey, basketball, and softball. Her cheeks were always red and she moved her head endlessly as she talked. Some girls loved her, usually the ones who played sports well. I didn't mind her, but by the end of the class, I was ready for Rathbone's mysterious silences.

Miss LeBlond had the smallest teeth I'd ever seen in an adult's face. As she talked, her head bobbing up and down, I watched her little pearly teeth. I wondered if you could model teeth. People model their legs and their hands. Gus could be a hand model. He has big square hands. Even the ends of his fingers are square.

Right from the beginning of the course, Miss LeBlond tried to stop us from giggling.

"Girls, this subject is of utmost importance to you."

"What does utmost mean?" Carol-Lee called out. Her voice was high and loud and if you didn't answer her, she'd repeat the question again and again.

"Utmost means very most, greatest. Anyway, Hygiene touches on your personal health and your procreative abil-

24

ity, and on your entire physical well-being. And those of you who play sports," she paused to smile at the athletes, "know how crucial physical well-being is."

Sure enough, Carol-Lee blared out, "What does procreative mean?"

"It means reproductive, your ability to reproduce, to have babies. Hygiene affects beauty, girls. I don't need to tell you how important that is. I can't promise you that staying attentive in Hygiene will improve your love life, but it might."

The front row laughed and looked sideways at each other. The Cynthias rolled their eyes to the ceiling. Morna, who thought she was the most beautiful girl in the class ever since she'd been picked to play Snow White in fourth grade, checked her reflection in the glass cabinet doors.

I studied the pattern of the owl's wing feathers as Miss LeBlond discussed leafy green vegetables and the pores of your skin. Carol-Lee interrupted every few minutes. "Is cabbage a leafy green vegetable?" "How does sweat come out the pores?" "I heard that if you squeeze a pimple on your face anywhere above your mouth you can get a brain infection." Carol-Lee didn't even mean to be funny.

I practiced drawing the owl, trying to get the feathers right. When I'd finished the owl, I thought I'd work on a sketch of the hawk. It made me feel better to know I had something to do during the class. I could just sketch all year. The back table was far enough away from the front of the room that Miss LeBlond would never notice. Catherine was drawing horses. From sitting beside her in so many classes now, I knew she specialized in horses. Horses

25

running. Horse heads with manes flying in the wind. Horses jumping over stone walls. Mares and foals. She always named her pictures, writing in block letters under each. Star, Midnight, Chestnut, Beauty. I suggested some new names. "How about Whiskey? Or Raisin?" Catherine glanced down at the drawing, frowning as if I'd made an obvious mistake. She did use Raisin under one picture. But then she went right back to her usual style: Blackie, King, Velvet, Lady.

After two weeks on skin care and food types, Miss LeBlond started in on the real stuff. She placed a plastic human torso on the front counter. It looked so pink and shiny, garish in front of the faded chart of the elements on the wall. Without a head, arms, or legs, the torso reminded me of a giant block of Spam, and my dismembered Barbie Doll. On the other side, Miss LeBlond propped up a chart of the monthly cycle.

"Do you have your period yet?" Catherine whispered.

I shook my head.

"Me, neither. My mother was really late, so I probably will be, too."

"Miss LeBlond, I already have my period, so I know all this stuff." It was Carol-Lee, of course. Ten or twelve arms waved. Everyone who had their period wanted to make sure that the rest of us knew it. It was just like this last year with bras. Anyone who wore one made sure that a strap slipped when everyone else would see.

I was drawing the owl's feet, skinny and curved, scaly, too, with hooked claws. Catherine was drawing horses' legs running and standing still. "Do horses get periods?" I whispered.

"Ask Miss LeBlond."

"You ask her."

"No, you. You thought of it. Come on. I dare you."

"Darers go first. I'll give you my dessert if you do it." We usually had brownies on Wednesdays.

Catherine raised her hand. I hunched down over my drawing. "Do horses get periods?" she said.

"Excuse me?" Miss LeBlond sounded hopeful that she'd misunderstood the question.

"Do horses get periods?" Catherine made it sound like an eager, innocent question that had just floated into her mind.

"Right, and they wear Maxi-pads," said Cynthia One.

Miss LeBlond, flustered, shot a frown at Cynthia, and fumbled for an answer. "Catherine, dear, I really don't know. Maybe you could research it and get back to us with what you learn."

Catherine nodded, then looked back down. She glanced over at me, and I started laughing silently. Keeping it inside made it worse. My shoulders heaved and my eyes watered. I tried not to look at Catherine but I could feel her shoulders shaking, too. "You win," I whispered.

When I got home that afternoon, I thought about telling Gus what happened. He's great at keeping a straight face. But I felt embarrassed mentioning periods.

I picked up my notebook and climbed the stairs to the Llewellyns', knocked our old code—one-pause-two-pause-three—and walked in. Sebastian's rain boots were lying in the hall where he'd pulled them off. Gus's hooded sweatshirt hung from the closet doorknob and his hockey stick was propped in the corner next to a soccer ball. The air smelled like toast, wet sneakers, and laundry detergent. Except for Carol, the Llewellyns had an all-male house, so different from my all-female house.

Downstairs, with just me, Mom, and Emma, the rooms were always neat. No one left shoes in the living room or T-shirts on the dining-room table. Emma would explode. Downstairs the coffee table was always bare, the wood polished weekly with lemon oil. Mom brought fresh flowers every Friday and set them in a green glass vase on the mantel or in a blue bowl on the table in front of the bay window.

Upstairs, the mantel was cluttered with Matt's softball trophy, a Lego sculpture that Sebastian refused to take apart, Gus's soccer team schedule and Carol's abandoned knitting. The coffee table was always hidden under newspapers, magazines, and at least one coffee mug, usually several days old. Occasionally Carol would start a clean-up campaign, and she'd buy flowers and wash the slip-covers and the curtains. But then she'd get involved in an article or a new proposal and gradually the clutter would creep back and she'd just shake her head and go back to her study, which was just as messy as the rest of the house.

Even our bathrooms were different. At the Llewellyns', the toilet seat was usually up. Sometimes the room smelled minty from Matt's shaving cream. He had a little brush that he dabbed it on with. When we were little, Gus and I would sit on the edge of the tub and watch Matt shave. He'd dab white beards on us with the little brush. It tickled. Then Matt would lift us up so we could see our beards in the mirror. Their medicine cabinet had things I'd never seen before—ointment for muscle pulls, athlete's-foot powder, and Carol's facial mud, gray-brown in a green jar. Gus said when she put it all over her face and let it dry she looked like a medicine man from the Amazon rain forest. Our medicine cabinet had talcum powder, eyedrops, headache pills, hand lotion, and mouthwash. Our house smelled lemony. Their house smelled sweaty and spicy, like men.

Gus was up on the top floor working on a model rocket. His worktable was an old door lying on two sawhorses. When he saw my notebook, he found his under a pile of *Mad* magazines and we sat on the window seat in our writing spots.

"Hi, Teresa."

"Hi, Vortrum."

I leaned back, opened the notebook to a fresh page, and started over.

> Teresa, known to her friends as Terry, is fifteen. She has red hair and green eyes. Her favorite color is blue. Her favorite food is ice cream. She's very smart and especially likes to study languages. She is five feet, two inches tall. For fun, she rides her bike and reads. You can recognize her by the little freckle above her left eyebrow.

29

When I looked up, Gus had also paused. "Let's read each other's," he said.

"Mine's dumb. I just got started."

"Come on, Miranda, it's just so we get an idea of the character. That way maybe we'll get plot ideas."

I didn't want to, but I handed him the notebook. He handed me his.

Vortrum, Rocket Patrol Training Cadet, gazed down at the tiny creature in his hand. "Jellub, I can't take you with me. No pets allowed at the training academy. I know you'll miss me, but for your own safety you must wait here with my parents, until I return." He placed the little ball of fur back in the carved wooden box it preferred for its bed. "You'll feed him, won't you, Mother? I won't put him in danger. No, Mother, don't cry now. I'll be all right." Vortrum's mother dried her eyes on the edge of her silver cape. He kissed her gently on the cheek, shook hands with his father, pulled his sister's braid, and left the dome tic unit.

I read it twice. I didn't know what to say, it was so much better than my boring stuff. When I looked up, Gus was tapping his front teeth with his pencil. "I like that freckle," he said. "But the rest is kind of dull. Doesn't she *do* anything? Make her clean her room or something."

"Cleaning your room is interesting?"

30

"You can show us what she keeps in her room. That will tell about her."

I nodded. What would she have? A canopy bed? When I was younger, I'd always wanted one, white with lace, and a dressing table. I never figured out what you did with a dressing table, but the bride magazines I used to look at always had them. No, she wouldn't have such stupid fancy stuff. I had to get her in shape, make her more interesting.

"I like Vortrum's pet. What is he?"

"I don't know. I just made him up."

"What'll we do next?"

"Keep writing."

"I think I'll start over," I said. I ripped out the page I'd written. Now I knew why Gus liked spiral notebooks: you can rip out pages without wrecking them. I picked the little paper ends out of the spiral, then started again.

> Terry reached for the scissors and hacked off her braids. Her red hair frizzed up around her head. She'd wanted to do that for a long time. Next, she pulled the lace canopy down from her bed. I'm tired of this frilly junk, she said to herself. I want to have some fun. She decided to change her clothes. She took off the pink sweater and skirt and put on her jeans and a baggy black T-shirt. She kicked off her black flats, too, and put on purple hightops. She even stuffed the pink outfit in the wastebasket. Then she got on her bike and rode off, looking for something to do.

31

I gave my new version to Gus. He handed me his. Gus had sent Vortrum into space.

Vortrum's first assignment was to patrol the fledgling colony, Earth. It wasn't a dangerous mission, just routine, right for a training cadet. But Vortrum hoped something exciting would happen. No sooner had he clamped his seat straps, checked his helmet, signaled to the control tower, and taken off, than he heard a familiar sound, a low humming noise. "Jellub, how did you get in here?" The tiny creature peeked out from behind the seat, wiggling its ears. "I bet you hid in my knapsack, didn't you? You aren't supposed to be here. It's dangerous." Jellub hummed on a higher note. "No, you're not supposed to take care of me. I'm a cadet. I'm supposed to take care of myself." The little creature made a low hum, and curled up next to Vortrum's seat. The cadet scratched his own pointed ear. This mission was off to an unusual start.

When I looked up, Gus was writing in my notebook.
"Hey, what're you doing?"
"Keeping the story going. You can write in mine if you like."
"I'll wait and see what you're doing with Terry."
"Teresa."
"Terry is her name."
"That sounds like all those other dumb girl characters.

Make her Teresa. It sounds more like a real person. I like it when she cuts off her hair. Good action. Give her things to do."

"What if she just likes to sit around? Have lunch or take a nap?"

"Boring."

I looked back down at Gus's notebook. Vortrum was in his ship. I skipped a line and began to write. Who said sleep was boring?

> *Halfway to earth, Vortrum began to feel tired. Time for his dinner and then sleep. He'd been in the air for seven hours and he'd passed twelve stars, two space colonies, and one rocket bus. He put the ship on automatic steering, turned on the radar alarm, and took off his seat straps. Jellub woke up and stretched his back. He cleaned his pointy nose and claws with his tongue. Vortrum opened the foil dinner-pouch and gave Jellub one of the tablets. They chewed them slowly. When all ten tablets were gone, Vortrum lay on the cabin cot and fell asleep. Jellub curled up next to his feet. The ship, in the darkness of space, sped closer and closer to Rodon, the mystery planet, protected by radar invisibility.*

"Let's trade back," Gus said, and handed back my notebook.

His little pencil writing filled a full page.

Teresa biked down the hill towards Main Street.
She had her birthday money in the pocket of her jeans.
Next to the candy store, she saw five teenagers leaning
against the wall. They all had black clothes and strange
haircuts. Behind them was a hairdresser's shop. SNIP-
SNAP, *the sign said. The window showed pictures of*
haircuts just like the five teenagers had. Teresa locked
her bike to the signpost and went inside. "Dye it black
and make it unusual," she told the hairdresser.

Wait, Teresa was my character. "You can't do that. I
like her red hair. You're going to give her a Mohawk, aren't
you?"

"No, I thought one of those cuts where one side is
shaved, and it's all dyed black."

"Forget it. I like her hair the way it is. Whoever makes
up a character gets to decide what happens to her."

"Vortrum's going to land his ship in her town so they
can meet. I like this part about the mystery planet. Maybe
you could make up more about that. Okay, skip the haircut. If you don't like it, cross it out."

I checked my watch. "I've got homework," I said. "See
you tomorrow." I took my notebook with me, just in case
Gus thought of something even stranger to add.

5

I didn't think it was possible for Miss Ayers to inflict anything dumber than Hygiene on us, but I was wrong. The third Thursday in September, when we walked into class, Miss Rathbone was standing with a woman who looked as if she'd dressed up early for Halloween.

She was at least six feet tall, even in flat shoes. She had on a silver dress with a full skirt and scooped neck that showed a ladder of knobby bones down the center of her chest. Her arms were pipe-cleaner thin, like Olive Oyl's. At her waist, she wore a pink satin sash, tied in a bow like a little girl's party dress. Around her neck she wore a chiffon scarf, pink, of course. Her cheeks were pink, too, big circles of pink. Her eyes were outlined in black and above each eyelid was a splotch of sparkly silver. But strangest of all was her hair. I'd never seen hair that orange. I bet it glowed in the dark. It looked scratchy, like steel wool, and she had it pulled into a lump on the top of her head that looked as if it might explode any time. Beside her, Miss Rathbone looked like a black-and-white photo, in her gray dress and black orthopedic oxfords. "Girls, let me introduce Miss Leopold, your dancing teacher."

"Delighted to meet you," the tall woman said. Her voice squeaked, and her flowery perfume drifted through the classroom. Some girls tried to fan it away, but Miss Rathbone gestured for them to stop.

"You'll have dance class every week on Friday afternoon instead of study hall," Miss Rathbone said. I loved her calm, low voice. The class clapped at the news of no study hall. That was before we knew what dance class was like.

The next afternoon we filed into the assembly hall and gathered near the stage, not knowing what to do. Miss Leopold sailed in the door carrying a record player and a stack of records. She had on the same outfit she'd worn when Miss Rathbone introduced her, except the scarf was white with silver stars. Catherine and I carefully maneuvered to a spot on the farthest edge of the group.

After plugging in the record player, Miss Leopold stood on the stage, with her big feet pointing out in first position and her arms in front of her in a stiff circle. "Girls, girls, we are going to have the most delicious time each week," she gushed. She had no eyebrows, just pencil lines. Did she shave them or pluck them out? It looked painful. "It is ab-so-lute-ly im-per-a-tive, my darlings, that you carry your-selves with poise at all times. Heads up. Shoulders back. Derrières tucked. Tummies in." Of course there were a few giggles. Miss Leopold laughed along in a high falsetto. She showed us the waltz and made us try it, dancing in pairs. Catherine and I grabbed each other in desperation. If we had to do this, at least we could do it together instead of with people we hated. Miss Leopold circled the room cor-recting us.

I remembered a song that Gus liked to sing. He'd heard it on the folk station his father listened to. It described Uncle Walter who loved to go waltzing with bears. When-ever Gus sang it I could imagine Uncle Walter, a chubby bald-headed old guy in overalls and workboots, sneaking out the back door and following the path into the woods at night to join a group of big, brown, furry bears. Together they'd sway and turn. One, two, three, one, two, three. Half-lumbering, half-graceful, they'd dance with their eyes closed, holding each other gently. "He loved to go waltzing, wa-wa-wa-waltzing. He loved to go waltzing, waltzing with bears."

Listening to Miss Leopold, I thought of a class of bears. "Now, bears," Miss Leopold would say in her high, stuffy-nose voice. "Walk naturally, heads high, graceful, graceful, and smile, darlings, smile." She'd pat them on their rumps, trying to see if they were tucking in beneath all that fur. They'd shuffle across the shiny floor, shy little grins beneath their pointy noses.

The image made me smile. Luckily, Miss Leopold

couldn't read my mind. "Perfect, perfect, a lovely smile, darling."

After two circles around the hall, we gathered in front of the stage again. Except for the handful of girls who always won blue cooperation ribbons on awards day, the class looked as enthusiastic as a police lineup. "Girls, please now, give me your ve-ry fullest attention. Next, the fox-trot, a useful step, always a useful step. Who shall be my partner?"

No one volunteered. I bent my knees, hiding behind the girls in front of me. She pointed to Sandra, who had the misfortune of being the tallest girl in the class. "Come forward, my dear."

Sandra walked slowly toward the front, scratching her head.

"Please, dear, we do not scratch in public. It simply is not done, not in polite society." As we learned over the following months, polite society was one of Miss Leopold's favorite terms. In polite society we do not scratch or burp. We always smile and even curtsy sometimes. I couldn't imagine ever having to curtsy. But we practiced it anyway, a six-point curtsy, six long counts to the floor and six back up, my thighs aching the whole time.

I told my mother how useless it was but she didn't agree with me. "It's important to have some social graces. You'll see when you're older. Manners are impressive."

"When am I going to do a six-point curtsy?"

"When you meet the queen," she said, without a smile. For a woman lawyer, she's surprisingly old-fashioned sometimes.

Every Friday, when we had dance class, Miss Leopold would pick her victim. She always wore a dress with a full skirt and a matching scarf. She had cold sweaty hands, like iced fish. Beneath a layer of peppermint, her breath was sour. Not only did you worry about where to hold on and how to avoid stepping on her feet—your hard-soled school shoes crunching down on her soft slippers—but you knew everybody else was watching, happy it wasn't their turn.

After Miss Leopold demonstrated the step, we had to try it ourselves while she watched. The record player sometimes revolved too slowly, making the music drone. Dance class was the worst. At least in Hygiene I could draw.

After a few weeks of dance class, Miss Leopold turned off the record player early. "Gather around, my darlings. I have some ve-ry im-por-tant news for you." Miss Leopold waited for the group to circle around her. "As you probably know, this year you are old enough to attend the Junior Dances, a wonderful opportunity to practice your social skills. And of course," she paused deliberately, smiling coyly, "you will meet young men."

Cynthia's group leaned their heads together to whisper.

"What schools are the boys from?" asked Morna, who plucked her eyebrows and insisted that *Seventeen* was too babyish for her.

"St. Stephen's, The Winchell School, Munroe Prep, maybe others."

This set more girls whispering, comparing who they knew. I didn't know anybody at those places, except maybe

39

Hugh, my mother's college roommate's son. I used to call him Pee-Hugh when we were little, and it made him cry. He went to Winchell when he was younger, but his mother might have shipped him further away now.

"The first dance is the week before Thanksgiving. We'll be sending out a registration form at the beginning of next week, but I thought you might want to tell your parents the exciting news yourselves."

I knew my mother would sign me up for all three. I'd have to get a dress, stockings, the works. Probably a haircut. And dance with some stranger with bad breath who'd tramp all over my feet.

"You won't catch me at one of those," Catherine whispered.

I raised my hand. "Can anyone else come?" I asked.

"Do you mean, may you bring a guest? Yes, you may invite a friend, but you must give me his name beforehand." Miss Leopold gave me one of her coy smiles. I was just thinking about inviting Gus. I could teach him the steps and we could bring a pack of cards and play gin rummy if we got tired of trying to dance. If Gus would come, I knew I'd be able to stand it. Friends do things for each other, I'd remind him.

It started to rain as school let out. I just made it onto the bus before it poured. The driver let me off at the end of the block because it's one way the wrong way. The sidewalk was one long puddle. My shoes squelched every time I took a step. I put my backpack on top of my head and ran, but still the rain dripped down my neck.

"Take yourself right into a hot shower. Leave those wet

things in there and we'll sort them out once you're dry," Emma said.

I love the way sweatpants feel after you've been cold or wet.

Emma had made real hot chocolate while I was in the shower, the kind where you heat the cocoa, sugar, and salt together, then add the milk, and she put out a plate of my very favorite cookies, too, shortbread squares. Emma knows about comfort. She sat at the table with me, knitting a tiny yellow sweater for her niece's baby. Yellow's good for boys or girls. Emma's clever that way.

"Catherine has the nicest hair, Emma, dark and curly. She calls it a Brillo bush. She says she wants to get it cut so short it can't curl, but her mother won't let her. It's not like Brillo at all, it's more like a poodle."

"Nothing wrong with your own hair," Emma said.

"I didn't say there was. I just like Catherine's, that's all. And she has beautiful eyes, too, Emma. You can't see them when she wears her glasses but they're almost purple, like those candles in the little glasses at your church. She's really tall. Not as tall as Gus, but taller than me by a couple of inches. She's so funny, Emma. She does this imitation of Rathbone—"

"Miss Rathbone."

"—of Miss Rathbone that cracks me up. She puts her hands behind her back and slides her glasses down so they're hanging on the end of her nose, just like Rathbone, Miss Rathbone, does. Then she walks back and forth, very slowly, sort of hunched forward, and she gets her voice so low. It's great."

41

Emma didn't smile at the description. She has ideas about teachers and respect. "Since you like her so much, why don't you invite her over?"

I called Catherine and she said she could come over Saturday. If the rain stopped, we'd ride bikes. If it kept up, we'd go to a movie or something. "You don't have to pick me up," she said. "I'll ride my bike or take the bus if it's raining. It's not that far."

Emma sniffed when she heard that. She wasn't used to my being old enough to get around the city on my own.

I slept over at Gus's Friday night as I did on lots of Fridays. We always watched old horror movies on Theater of Thrills. Matt, Gus's father, watched with us. His favorite movie was *The Spider Woman's Web*. Mine was *The Mummy's Revenge*, and Gus liked *Vampire Feast*. Sebastian couldn't stay up that late, and he might get nightmares anyway. Carol hated the scary music, so she put her Walkman on and read in bed.

Once in a while, but very seldom, Gus slept over at my house. It wasn't as much fun, since Emma made us go to bed at ten. There was also the risk of stewed tomatoes at dinner, and even sometimes brussels sprouts. Gus tried not to hold it against me. "Check the menu," he'd say. But Emma was secretive about vegetables. One night, Gus sat through the whole dinner with four brussels sprouts tucked in above his gums, two on each side. Naturally, he didn't say much. I thought he looked lumpy, but Emma didn't notice.

"Why does she make you eat that stuff? Turnips, as-

42

paragus, brussels sprouts? They're more disgusting than milk of magnesia."

I could have told Gus about the dance that night. We were watching Theater of Thrills and trying to shoot pieces of popcorn into each other's mouths. A ring of kernels surrounded us. Matt had fallen asleep on the couch. He had a cold. All evening he'd been sucking gray lozenges that stank like mothballs. "The real stuff," he said when we asked how he could stand eating those things. I tried one and had to spit it out.

Vampire Vamp was on Theater of Thrills. The vampire lured men to her house and killed them in the usual vampire way. When she went to a dance at the castle and the duke danced with her, you could tell he was done for.

"He's next," Gus said.

"They're doing the fox trot," I said.

"She'll get him when he takes her home."

"That's a waltz."

"What're you talking about?" Gus asked.

"The dance steps. I learned them at school."

I was about to bring up the dance, but Gus said, "Sshh, the police chief saw them dance past the mirror and the duke's arms were empty."

I didn't get another chance to ask Gus about the dance that night.

The rain blew away before morning, leaving the wind behind. Every last leaf had fallen off the trees in front and the wind kept the branches shaking. When Catherine arrived, her hair was blown into a tangle and her nose was red.

"The wind almost knocked me off my bike a few times. It's wild." She pulled off her windbreaker and tried to smooth her hair. It popped right back up.

"Come upstairs and meet my friend Gus."

Carol poked her head out of the kitchen when she heard a new voice. "Nice to meet you, Catherine. Gus's upstairs, Miranda. See if you can get him to go out. It's too nice to stay inside all day."

Adults always want to air kids out as if we were rugs.

Gus was sitting on his window seat writing. "I'm doing Vortrum's childhood. He learned to read by the time he was three by studying cereal boxes. His favorite words were crunchy and delicious. If he liked something a lot, he called it crunchy. His father taught him two other space languages before he started school."

Catherine looked around the room. "You build models?" she said. "My cousin Dennis makes rockets. Have you built any multistage?"

Gus looked up. "Not yet, but I ordered a kit." He rummaged around on his desk and found the catalogue to show her.

"Want to come bike riding with us?" I asked Gus, expecting him to say no. He seldom came along when I had friends over. I didn't come over when his friends were around much, either.

"Where are you going?"

"Along the Charles River," Catherine said. "It will be fun with the wind."

Gus agreed, so we made lunches and set off single file. The wind was so strong we couldn't talk once we got to the river path. I was glad Emma insisted I bring gloves. Gus was in front at first, then Catherine. I stayed behind. I hate having to worry that I'm holding people back.

We went way up the river where the bike path curves far away from the road and trees line the riverbank. In a pine grove, we sat down on the soft needles, out of the wind. I leaned against a tree and looked up at the crisscross of branches high over my head. Way up, the wind shook the tops of the trees, but down in the middle of the grove, it was calm. Catherine's dark hair fuzzed around her face. Gus offered her one of his Lorna Doones. I wondered if he liked her.

In school on Monday, Catherine didn't mention Gus, or ask me stupid questions about him, or drop his name a lot the way people do when they decide they like someone. I was relieved. If they started liking each other, who would I be friends with?

During study hall, I remembered to check the ginkgo tree. It was bare—I'd missed the leaves falling again. It's hard to catch things while they're changing. Maybe the only way to see it would be to sit under the ginkgo and let the tree cover me with little yellow fans. That way I wouldn't miss it.

6

The next week at school, I had two projects assigned. For Hygiene, I could choose between a chart and a report. I liked charts and diagrams, making everything line up and look clear and simple even when it wasn't. The English assignment was much harder. As soon as Miss Rathbone gave it, I knew immediately who I'd write about.

Rathbone never gave out assignments on a piece of paper, or wrote them down on the board. She gave them out loud, walking back and forth with her hands behind her back, spinning the assignment out, as if thinking it up right then, as she said it. I loved to watch her walk. Even though she stooped, she glided, smooth, light, and limber. Her eyes drilled into you, knowing you without words. Most of the class was afraid of her. They called her Hawk-eye, the Witch, Hunchback. But she didn't scare me. I wanted to be just like her. Not old or hunched over, but sharp, low-voiced, fast and fearless. I even thought she was beautiful. She was old, but she had this glow when she smiled.

"I'm asking you this time to write a profile of someone you know very well, someone you know almost as well as you know yourself. Pick someone you can observe. Be a sneak, a detective—good writers have to be snoops. Be nosy. Follow your subject around. Notice the way she eats, what she does with her hands when she's sitting, her fa-vorite clothes, any possessions that are especially impor-tant. Make us interested in this person. Make her come alive. Use everything you already know and find out more."

I chose Gus of course, and I got started that afternoon. Gus had to watch Sebastian. I said I'd help, figuring I could observe without him noticing. "Let's take him to the aquar-ium," Gus said.

Since it was a weekday we found a spot by the rail of the penguin pool. The little guys were diving off rocks, swimming underwater without moving a flipper, then climbing back out again and barking at their success.

Gus held Sebastian up so he could see over the rail. He still wore the Mickey Mouse watch he'd bought when he was nine. Walking up the ramp that circled the big tank, we stopped to see the fish swim past.

Gus loved the turtles. "Here he comes again," he said as one of the big guys drifted by, big wrinkled legs almost touching the glass. Gus made a turtle face, his upper lip pulled down and his eyes half-shut, his shoulders bent forward as if he wore a shell. He moved his head slowly from side to side, but the turtles drifted by without a blink.

I kept notes on Gus for a week. His favorite clothes were jeans, sweatshirts, high-topped sneakers with the original Gus Llewellyn lace design, and his father's old leather jacket from college, frayed at the cuffs. He ate any kind of chips, garlic pickles that he bought at the corner deli, popcorn with salt and butter, vanilla yogurt, and Lorna Doones. He always ate Lorna Doones the same way, biting around the edges. "I leave the airplane for last," he said.

I couldn't describe his laugh. I didn't want to make him sound like a maniac. He had a loud laugh, an explosion. When he thought something was really funny, his face got red and his eyes watered. Even when I didn't find something funny, Gus's laugh made me laugh.

I tried to put all the details together in my profile but it sounded like any kid who wore jeans and ate cookies. Even the part about rockets, stars, and space sounded corny and ordinary. Catherine let me read a draft of her profile on her father. It started, "He has seven library cards in his wallet and he uses them all." After that, I worked on a catchy opening line for Gus.

For Hygiene, I made a chart of male and female development at six, twelve, and eighteen, copying the details from the encyclopedia. Emma must have seen it on my desk when she was cleaning the house. I bet that's what got her started on the lecture. She called it a talk, but it was a lecture. First Miss LeBlond and then Emma! Everyone wanted to talk about sex. What could I say: I don't want to hear any more?

I was sitting at Mom's desk working on *Alien Attraction*. She lets me use her desk as long as I don't touch the stuff in the drawers and cubbies, or take her pens. Emma called to me from the kitchen. "Are you busy?"

"Let me finish this paragraph." I was describing Teresa's childhood. I gave her a big family, eight kids, and made her the youngest. Her father was an electrician. I was proud of myself for thinking that up. Vortrum might need tools later if he had to rig up some connection to his planet, and maybe Teresa could know some electronics, too. It might be useful. I finished the page and put my notebook in my room.

Emma was scraping chopped onions into a pot. They'd made her eyes tear. "Fill the teapot, Miranda, please," she said. She wiped her hands on the front of her apron, patted her eyes with a paper towel, and sat down at the kitchen table with me.

"We need to talk." Emma never wasted time leading up to a subject. "About woman things, if you know what I mean. I'm talking about babies." She looked at me quickly, then looked away. "Do you know how babies are made?" I thought of teasing her and saying, "At the factory," or "In the cabbage patch," but Emma's tone made me pause.

She seemed so uncomfortable I didn't want to make it any worse for her.

"They teach us in school, Emma, all about the egg and the sperm and everything."

Emma sniffed twice. "Those teachers probably aren't even married. There's more to it than that." She sipped her tea and cracked an oatmeal cookie in half. I knew she'd eat both halves eventually. "First of all, Miranda, when a girl becomes a woman, and it'll happen to you any time now, she's got to be careful." She paused and stared at me, sadly, I thought. "I won't mince my words. You're old enough to know. You've got to be careful of how you sit and dress, how you act. Men get ideas." Emma's eyebrows rose as she said this. "It's a woman's responsibility to keep a man under control." She patted the air in front of her as if calming it down.

Then she took another sip of tea and switched to periods. Her version was more confusing than Hygiene class. Emma called it "the curse," and talked about cramps, and showers. "Don't wash your hair or take a bath when you've got it. Showers only. Tea and heating pads will take care of the cramps."

It sounded like an illness. I didn't understand about not taking a bath, but she switched the subject again before I could ask. "Did they talk about the marriage act at school?" She didn't wait for my answer, but rushed on as if trying to get through something unpleasant. It took me a few seconds to realize she was talking about sex. She never said it straight out. "It's a woman's duty, Miranda.

We all get used to it. Nobody likes to talk about this, but at first it does hurt. Luckily women are made to bear pain. It's a woman's duty." She nodded her head, punctuating the end of the talk. "That's enough of that. You'll learn more when you're older."

Pain? I hadn't heard about pain in Hygiene class or in the book that Mom gave me. How much did it hurt, and why? I could tell that Emma didn't want to discuss it further. I had to think of someone to ask. Maybe Catherine.

"I'll go finish my homework," I said.

Emma smiled and patted my hand. "Good girl."

Back on my desk, the Hygiene chart stood propped up against the wall. I lay it flat, took out markers and began to color in the letters. The bodies I'd drawn on the chart were paper dolls: perfect, no pain or problems, no confusion. I kept on coloring until dinner. But Emma's warnings drifted in and out of my head. I couldn't push them completely away. It was even too embarrassing to ask Catherine. Besides, she probably didn't know either.

On Thursday, I handed in the chart, and Friday afternoon Miss Leopold taught us the cha-cha.

"Girls, only one month remains before the dance. I need your very fullest cooperation."

She fluttered back and forth across the stage like a giant mutant butterfly, black and yellow. She was determined to drum in the basics before Thanksgiving. Box step, fox trot, waltz, I couldn't keep them straight. They all had jerky little steps that repeated over and over. Only when the music was playing did it vaguely make sense. Three people in the class could do the steps smoothly, with confidence. The rest of us bumped together like boats tied to the same mooring.

But Miss Leopold stayed cheerful, her hair in her bun, and her yellow chiffon scarf drifting lightly behind her as she demonstrated the steps one more time.

"Backs straight, tummies in, derrières tucked now, ladies. Small steps. Lightly, lightly, step *gently*. One, two, three, *one*, two, three. Gracefully, young ladies, please, be graceful."

As usual, I was dancing with Catherine. She hated dance class even more than Hygiene.

"One, two, puke. One, two, puke," Catherine kept muttering.

"That's disgusting," I hissed.

"No, *this* is disgusting," Catherine said. "Name me one reason why we have to learn this junk."

"So we can go to the Thanksgiving dance."

"We *want* to go to the Thanksgiving dance? Not me. Are you going?"

I nodded. "My mother thinks it's important to know these things for later, when we're grown-up." We'd had an argument about it when the letter arrived. Mom insisted that I go to all three dances, all three! I told her I'd hate it, and I'd go but I wouldn't dance. I'd hide in the bathroom. She didn't answer.

"Grown-ups don't do this," Catherine said. "Hockey players do it. People in the Roller Derby do it. But normal adult people don't go bumping each other in time to music."

"It's not supposed to be like this, idiot. The bumps aren't part of the dance."

Catherine let her mouth hang open in shock. "Now you tell me!"

"Sshh, Leopold has her eye on us. She's looking for a partner for the demonstration." I steered us to the far side of the room just as Miss Leopold swooped into the middle of the class and touched Anne-Marie's shoulder.

"Come in close, girls, and form a nice circle. I'm going to show you the cha-cha."

Miss Leopold turned on the music and demonstrated alone, sashaying up and back, knees high, hips swinging to the music. "One, two, *cha, cha, cha,*" she sang out, her hands at her waist pushing her skinny hips out left and right. Then she made Anne-Marie do it with her. Anne-Marie tried to freeze her face. I wasn't sure if she was hiding tears or laughs. "One, two, *cha, cha, cha,*" Miss Leopold drilled, dragging and pushing Anne-Marie. "Now everybody try it right where you are. One, two, *cha, cha, cha.* One, two, cha, cha, cha."

We moved two steps forward, slogged three steps in place, then stepped back two steps and slogged the three cha-cha-chas again.

"This is a step with spirit, girls. Listen to the music. Imagine yourselves on a tropical island." Then we teamed up with our partners and chugged up and back again and again.

"Sway like palm trees, ladies, graceful, graceful," said Miss Leopold.

"I didn't show my mother the invitation. I took it out

of the mail," Catherine whispered. "I don't think she'll find out."

I was trying not to step on Catherine's toes when I went forward. Miss Leopold had added arm movements to go with the hips. She looked like Chiquita Banana.

"I might try to talk Gus into coming with me since I have to go."

"Do you think he'll do it?"

"I don't know. He doesn't know how to dance."

Catherine began to do the steps extra hard, pounding the *one-two*s as if she were marching, folding her arms for the cha-cha-cha and scowling, like a tough marine on patrol.

"If Gus comes I won't have to dance with a stranger. The Cynthias said they line you up by height and pair you off boy-girl, and you're stuck for half the night. If you bring someone, you don't have to get in line. I don't want to dance with people I don't know."

The record ended, and Miss Leopold patted her forehead with her hanky. "If you're shopping for the dance, remember, no long dresses. This is a tea dance. Party dresses are appropriate. If you're bringing a friend, be sure to give his name to me at least a week before the dance."

Catherine whispered, "I'd wear spiked hair and chains. Let me know if Gus says yes, okay?"

I didn't see why she cared. She already said she wasn't going to the dance.

I invited Catherine to sleep over that Friday night. Emma promised we'd have hamburgers, potatoes, and peas. No eggplant, no stewed tomatoes, definitely no brussels sprouts.

Catherine brought her overnight clothes to school in a duffel bag. It looked big enough for a week's stay, and I wondered what she had in there. "Stuff to fool around with," she said.

That afternoon, she unloaded everything onto the extra bed in my room. I'd taken off the pile of pillows and the giant panda that usually sits there. Mom's old boyfriend Bernie had won the panda for me at an amusement park we went to for my sixth birthday, when I ate too much cotton candy and threw up on the Ferris wheel.

Catherine had brought her jeans, a sweatshirt, sneakers, and a nightshirt that said PROPERTY OF THE BOSTON RED SOX on the front. She changed into her jeans immediately. The rest of the duffel was filled with makeup and magazines, a hair drier, curlers, a comb and brush, cans of mousse and hair spray, and a magnifying mirror. "We can play makeovers," Catherine said. She showed me her eyelash curler and a can of purple spray-on hair color. "I've got glitter eye shadow, too."

I opened the lipstick tubes, Scarlette Runner, Papaya Plum, and Sunset Orange. "We better wait until after dinner," I said. "Where'd you get all this stuff?"

"My cousin Judy from California came to visit last summer and she showed me everything. We went to a mall and bought most of this then. My mother got the orange lipstick as a free sample and she left it in the medicine cabinet for a year so I added it to the collection." Catherine opened the Papaya Plum lipstick and spread it on deftly, pouting for the mirror. She pinched her lips together three times. "That blots it." Then she brushed on white powder in the space below each eyebrow. I hoped Emma wouldn't notice.

We went out for a walk before dinner. I showed her the park and the playground, and the little row of stores nearby. "When's Gus getting home?" she asked. I had no idea. He probably had a soccer game.

After dinner, we went into my room and closed the door. Catherine moved my reading lamp onto the dresser and put the desk chair in front of the mirror. "Sit down," she said. "I'm going to change your hairstyle."

I looked at my plain straight hair. I felt like Teresa about to be attacked by Gus's imagination.

"You go first," I said, giving Catherine the chair.

She got one side of her hair to stand up straight with mousse. It smelled like paint remover, and the liquid blush smelled like dead flowers. I opened the window, wondering how I'd sleep with the fumes in the room. I tried the eyelash curler but all it did was dent my lashes in a ninety-degree angle. At least it didn't hurt or pull any out.

When Catherine was finished, she read magazine advice columns out loud to me about how to make a boy notice you. I was bored. I thought of Gus and Matt upstairs, making popcorn and getting ready to watch Theater of Thrills. Maybe we could go up.

"Want to watch a horror movie?" I asked. "It's *The Cat Woman's Claws* tonight."

"I hate the music. It gives me chills. I'll watch if you turn the sound off."

That meant staying downstairs. Gus and Matt would never turn off the music. Emma agreed to let us watch Theater of Thrills, but she looked sideways at Catherine's hair and makeup. "I hope that all washes off," she said. I was glad I hadn't put any makeup on. I didn't want another lecture.

Catherine and the Cat Woman looked a lot alike, except the movie was an old black-and-white print, and Catherine was colorful, especially the pink and purple around her eyes. The movie was silly with the sound off. After the first commercial, we started making up lines for the characters, and that was fun, finally. I wished Catherine hadn't brought her makeup.

The next morning as Catherine and I were leaving to ride bikes, we met Gus. He had on his soccer uniform and was carrying his cleats. Matt honked the horn to hurry him up, so he didn't have time to talk. I could tell Catherine was sorry he had to leave. She watched the car until it turned the corner.

We rode our bikes along the river to Cambridge. At the boathouse we crossed the bridge and pedaled toward Harvard Square. We walked up Brattle Street dodging college students. Catherine tugged on my jacket when we passed the discount bookstore. "Let's browse," she said.

We flipped through the magazines first, and we were turning the racks of postcards when Catherine whispered, "See that guy in the raincoat? He looks creepy."

I glanced over, pretending to check the clock behind the cash register. He looked ordinary to me—raincoat, baseball cap, jeans, and loafers. He wasn't too old, maybe thirty. He had dark-frame glasses and no beard.

"Let's move," Catherine hissed. "He's watching us."

I couldn't tell if she was kidding. I followed her back to the children's book corner. We sat on the floor trying all the sample pop-up books.

"He's in the New Age section," Catherine whispered. "He followed us."

"Maybe he's looking for a book."

Catherine shook her head as if I were hopeless. "I think he's a flasher. That's why he's got that raincoat on."

"Half the people in Harvard Square have raincoats on."

"Sshh, he might be listening. Let's go."

When we were out on the sidewalk Catherine shook out her arms and legs as if dusting herself off. "Ugh, what a creep."

"He was just some guy looking for a book. What's wrong with you?"

"Miranda, wake up! He was looking for a chance to flash at us. Let's get something to eat. I'll tell you what happened last summer. Then you won't think I'm crazy."

It happened when Catherine took the ferry to visit her cousins at their summer house. Her mother watched her get on board and waved good-bye as the boat pulled out. First she sat on the top deck looking at the gulls, but after a while she got thirsty and went downstairs to the food stand. That's when she saw the weirdo.

"He was waiting at the bottom of the stairs, standing

behind a post. He stepped out when I came down, and he had his pants open. He wanted me to see his penis. He was watching my face with this weird smile."

I was cracking a peanut shell with my teeth and I spit the whole thing out on the grass. "That's disgusting. Did that really happen, Catherine?"

She nodded and crossed her heart. "It happened. I swear on my grave it happened. As soon as I saw what he was doing, I ran back upstairs. I was still thirsty, so I used the staircase at the other end of the boat. When I was buying a soda, I saw him watching me again. One of the captains was ordering coffee, so I told him the man was bothering me. The captain said something to him and he stayed away from me after that. Later, I told my mom about it. She said it's not unusual—some weird men get a kick out of showing their penis to young girls. I think it's sick. I wish I'd said something to him like 'Put that worm away.'"

We laughed.

"Or you could say, 'Looking for the men's room?'" I said, and we laughed again.

Catherine said, "I should have said, 'Excuse me, your fly's open,' and pretended it was an accident. Or maybe just screamed, '*Gross!*' as loud as I could."

We laughed until our stomachs hurt. When I was little and scared of thunderstorms, Gus used to tell me jokes and get me to laugh while the thunder boomed. You never feel as afraid when you're laughing. I finally caught my breath. "I still don't see why anyone would do it," I said.

"Me, neither," Catherine said. "But they do."

7

I finished my profile of Gus on Sunday night, but I wasn't satisfied. I put all the details together but it still sounded bland. I let my mother read it. She sat on the couch with her legs crossed, chewing on the end of her pencil while I paced in front of the fireplace waiting for her opinion.

"I like the description of his hands. But you sound a little stiff, self-conscious."

I chewed on a piece of hair. "I wish I'd picked somebody else, like Emma. Maybe I should start again."

"That's crazy. You've spent a lot of time on this and it has some great details. Sometimes it's hard to write about someone you care about, that's all."

"I do like my opening line, 'His best friend is a girl and he doesn't care what anybody says about it,' " I said.

"Me, too," Mom said. "It's Gus."

I slipped into Rathbone's class two minutes late and fished out the profile. Miss Rathbone was watering the yellow chrysanthemums on the bookcase. She put the watering can down and walked slowly across the front of the room. Both windows were wide open, letting in cold air and the smell of rain and wet leaves. I took a deep breath, happy as always to be in Miss Rathbone's calm presence where the unexpected might happen any time.

"Profiles are due, I see. I've been looking forward to these," Miss Rathbone said, touching the tips of her fingers together and smiling. "Who would like to read first?" she asked.

Catherine volunteered, surprising me. She walked to the front and stood by the blackboard. "My father has seven library cards." She described how her father read, sitting in a chair by the window, his feet propped up on the sill. When he was reading he didn't hear the phone, or anyone's voice. He dog-eared the corners of pages to mark his place, even though he always told Catherine not to do it. I listened because Catherine was my friend, but the rest of the class jiggled their feet and doodled on their notebooks.

"Any questions for Catherine?" Miss Rathbone asked. No one raised a hand so Rathbone asked what kinds of books he liked to read, and then thanked Catherine.

Cynthia Two volunteered next. Of course, she wrote

about Cynthia One, who sat at her desk fixing the curls on her shoulder and glancing around to see if we were looking at her.

"My best friend has hair the color of honey and eyes as blue as blueberries," read Cynthia Two, whose real name was Amy. I drew a picture of a girl with eyes like squished round berries and passed it to Catherine. She added fangs and freckles. I had to cough when Cynthia Two, or Amy, described Cynthia One as kind and generous. Miss Rathbone frowned at me, but I couldn't help it, I'd swallowed wrong in surprise.

Rathbone called on me next. I've never liked to read out loud. My voice gets thin and my throat itches. I tried to stand up straight and read louder so no one would see how nervous I really was.

"Gus. His best friend is a girl and he doesn't care what anybody says about it."

Miss Rathbone nodded.

"I've known him since we were babies, but he's changed in thirteen years. He's as tall as his father already, and his hands are so wide they can reach around his little brother's waist." I described Gus's favorite place—his window seat, and his favorite food—Lorna Doones, and his hobby—outer space: reading and writing about it, and making model rockets. I described his green sneakers, his jokes, the way he hugged his mother. "Gus was my first friend and he's my best friend." I finished it there. I was going to add "and I don't care what anybody says about it," but that sounded as if I did care, so I took it out.

"Nicely done, Miranda. Good details," Miss Rathbone

said. "There's a lot of warmth in your piece. Any questions for Miranda, class?"

"Is that the boy who waits for the bus with you?" asked Morna. I nodded. "He's cute," she told the rest of the class. I could feel myself blush. She made Gus sound like my boyfriend.

Halloween was Tuesday of that week. Gus and I always went out trick-or-treating together. We took Sebastian along for a block or two, then dropped him off back at the house and kept going.

My mother had promised she'd try to get home early so she could see our costumes, but I didn't think she'd make it. Something usually came up, some new twist in a case, or some last-minute meeting. When I saw her sitting on the couch opening the mail, I hugged her. "Want to guess what I'm going to be?"

"A princess?"

I laughed. "Nobody over nine is a princess, Mom. Guess again."

"I give up. Go change. The suspense is too great."

In my room, I pulled on black tights and my leotard. I had dropped ballet in seventh grade, but the leotard still fit. I liked ballet until they started pointe. Everyone else in the class was excited but I hated the hard shoes. I was thinking about trying tap or jazz, but I hadn't done anything about finding a class. On top of the leotard I pulled on a black cardigan sweater so Emma wouldn't nag me about catching cold.

The costume slid easily over my head—two pieces of cardboard hinged at the top with tape and tied at the sides with ribbon. I had spotted a refrigerator box in the back alley and salvaged the cardboard. I'd cut out two matching rectangles, painted them white, and drew the Queen of Hearts on them, from the design on Emma's canasta cards. The Ace of Spades wasn't colorful. The Queen's dress had stripes and dots, and tiny hearts on the ruffle.

I coated my face with clown white, pulled my hair into a ponytail, and tied my sneakers. They didn't look great with the costume but I wanted to be comfortable if we were going to walk as far as Gus hoped.

When I went into the living room, Mom was reading the paper. Emma was downstairs filling baskets with miniature candy bars for trick-or-treaters. She came upstairs and sat in the rocker.

"Turn around and let us see both sides," Mom said. "I love the queen's face—she looks mysterious. Walk over to the window and back."

I felt self-conscious. The cards came down to the middle of my thighs and from then on, it was just my tights.

"You look like a dancer," Emma said. "Just like a Broadway dancer with the long legs."

"That worries me," my mother said. "Do you think it's all right to go out like that?"

It was practically time to leave. I could have worn jeans, but they'd look too bulky. "It's fine."

My mother raised her eyebrows. "I'm not sure, Miranda. Maybe you should cover up more. You're not a little girl anymore."

I hated being fussed over. So what if people saw my legs? Big deal. I had tights on. "Mom, I've seen kids wear less.

You know those cat costumes, with the collars and the ears? You just wear a leotard with those. Lots of girls do that."

"And catch their death of cold," Emma butted in.

"I'm going with Gus. We're not going to any strange places. Nobody's going to bother us. We're careful."

"I guess Gus is big enough to scare off hecklers. But I worry about kids being out at night. Even on Halloween, this is still the city."

"We'll be fine, Mom."

"Are you warm enough?" Emma asked, just as I knew she would.

I showed her my sweater. I could hear Gus and Sebastian coming down the stairs.

"You haven't eaten anything," Emma said.

"I'll eat afterward," I promised.

Sebastian bounced in, long rabbit ears wobbling. Carol had painted a nose and whiskers on his face. He cupped his hands in front of him like paws. The tail pinned to the back of his fuzzy pajamas wiggled when he hopped. Gus strolled in wearing his father's old dinner jacket, a black shirt and a narrow silver tie. A white gangster's hat was tipped over his eye, and some cards and fake bills stuck out of his pockets. His parents came in, too, and the grownups looked us over.

"Guess who we are," I said.

"The Queen of Hearts," said Matt. "That's easy."

"And a Mafia boss?" guessed Mom.

Gus shook his head. "We go together."

"A gambler," said Emma.

65

"Yup, a card shark," said Gus. "The card shark and the Queen of Hearts."

"Queenie, where did you get those gorgeous long legs all of a sudden?" Matt teased. "They're growing up on us, Frannie," he said to Mom.

"How does the bunny tie in?" Carol asked.

"For good luck," I said.

Emma, Mom, and the Llewellyns always sat on the steps and watched the kids go up and down the street. Emma wore a witch's hat every year and Matt wore a gorilla mask. Mom and Carol held the baskets of candy.

After only three blocks, Sebastian said, "I'm cold." He'd pulled off his ears because they itched, and he lugged his bag as if it held bricks instead of candy. He didn't complain when we dropped him back at the house. My mother had already gone in. Carol took Sebastian up to bed. Emma and Matt stayed on the top step with the candy in their laps.

"Be in by nine-thirty," said Matt, as Gus and I waved good-bye again.

"Let's try the hill," Gus said.

"That's far."

"Somebody up there gave away cider and homemade donuts last year. I'm thirsty."

"You can't eat homemade stuff. It might be poisoned. You're supposed to throw away anything that isn't wrapped. There might be razor blades or needles in it."

"Oh, come on," Gus said.

Gus is stubborn when he gets an idea. I tried to walk

66

fast but my costume flapped against my legs. When we finally reached the bottom of Ridge Street, only a few trick-or-treaters were still out. From a few blocks away I could hear screams and firecrackers popping. High-school kids, I thought.

"How late is it?" I asked.

"Eight-fifteen. Come on, I'll show you the house with the cider."

Four pumpkins sat on the porch railing, candles still flickering, and a scarecrow stuffed with real straw was propped up on the top steps. When Gus rang the bell, a deep voice said, "Welcome to Haunted Hill. Open the door and come right in. We are *thrilled* to see you." Then a scary laugh followed.

"It's a tape," Gus said, delighted. He opened the door. The hall glowed with purple light.

"Hello, dearies," said a lady vampire, filling cups with liquid from a black pot wreathed in wisps of steam.

"Dry ice," Gus showed me. "This is neat."

"Care for some brew?" asked the vampire, her long red nails holding the styrofoam cup. Gus took one but I shook my head. "Take something to eat." The vampire pointed at the plates on the table. Gus took a donut, but not me. I kept thinking of razor blades in apples. The donuts smelled delicious. I knew they were probably all right, but once you have a scary idea in your mind, it's hard to make it go away.

The next house had a light in one downstairs window. We climbed up a flight of stone stairs. When I rang the bell we heard the chimes inside, *da, da, da, dum*. After a few minutes, the door opened halfway and a gray-haired woman in a velvet jacket peered out at us, frowning.

"Trick or treat," we said together, holding out our bags.

"Aren't you too old to be out trick-or-treating? Halloween is for younger children." She didn't offer us anything for our bags. She acted as if we were trying to get away with something, cheat or steal.

"You're never too old to go trick-or-treating," Gus said. "My dad even goes with us sometimes."

"He should act his age," the woman said. "It's inappropriate. If I were you, I'd head home right away and get out of those outfits. Especially you, my dear," she said to me. "You're barely covered."

Gus laughed. "Barely covered." He loved puns.

She ignored him and shut the door.

"We better go home," I said.

"Don't let that witch spoil everything. She's crazy. Anyone can go trick-or-treating." He looked back up at the stone house. "She deserves a trick." He pulled the roll of toilet paper out of his coat pocket. "We'll decorate her bushes, and fill her mailbox."

We each had a roll to work with and we wove the paper in and out of the hedge branches on both sides of the steps. No one looked out the window. Gus gave me the shaving cream and I sprayed a pile of it inside her fancy mailbox and smothered the eagle on top. When we glanced back from across the street, it looked as if snow had fallen.

Gus checked his watch. "It's nine."

"I'm cold," I said.

We walked down the hill with our bags bumping against our legs. The streets were empty. Most of the pumpkins on people's porches had burned out, or been snuffed by the wind. A pumpkin lay in the middle of the road, smashed open with its face split apart. A block further, we saw another one, and some raw eggs splattered the windows of a parked car.

We walked faster. Halfway home I noticed three older boys crossing the street. The heels of their boots tapped loudly on the sidewalk as they walked up to us.

"Hey, kids, get a lot of stuff?" said the tallest. I couldn't tell if he was being friendly or not.

"We did okay," Gus answered.

I wished they'd just keep walking. They scared me with their slicked hair and boots. "Come on," I said to Gus.

"Don't talk to guys like us?" the shortest one said to me. "Afraid of the big boys?" he whined, making fun of me.

"Leave her alone," the tall one said. "She's just a kid."

"I'm not so sure," said the short one. "She might be just what I'm looking for."

I held my breath and closed my eyes for a second, wishing I could make him disappear. I reached for Gus's hand and held on tight. He squeezed it, letting me know I wasn't alone. But I was the one they were picking on, not him. Just because I was a girl. It made me mad. I should've worn jeans, I thought.

The middle-sized one touched the front of my costume, tracing the design with one finger. "Did you paint this?"

"Her mommy did it," the short one said.

69

"I did it myself," I said.

"Nice work. How old are you?" the middle-sized one said. His voice was softer than the short one's.

"I'll check," said the short one. He reached for the side of my costume but I stepped back, away from him. He held an edge of the cardboard and the costume ripped at the shoulder and side and the card slipped down, showing my sweater and leotard.

I moved behind Gus, clamping my teeth to keep from crying. In the light from the street lamp I could see a patch of purple acne on the short boy's cheek.

Gus kept me behind him. "Don't touch her," he said. He was a head taller than the short one.

"What—is she your girlfriend?" The short one gave a snort of a laugh.

I wanted to run. If he ever touched me, I'd throw up, I knew it.

"Let 'em alone," said the tallest one. "They're just kids. Come on, we're late enough."

"At least we can take their candy," the short one complained.

Gus pulled me off the curb. We started to run. My costume kept flapping and knocking against my legs. I tried to hold it, but it slipped. I sobbed as we ran. Gus kept hold of my hand the whole way. We didn't stop until our block. We leaned against a building, catching our breath. The street was quiet, no sound of boots.

The boy's words kept repeating in my mind, his voice a sneer. I covered my face with my hands, ashamed to let Gus see me cry.

70

Gus put his arm around me. I hid my face against his shoulder.

"What am I going to say about this? My costume's wrecked."

"Can we fix it?" Gus examined the ties. "We don't have to say how it happened. It could have just fallen apart. Take it off and wear my jacket. We'll carry it the rest of the way."

"You'll be cold," I said.

"We're almost home."

He helped me pull off the cardboard and held his jacket for me. I slipped my arms into the sleeves. It was huge, hanging halfway to my knees, the silky lining still warm from Gus.

We walked the last two blocks in silence, Gus carrying the Queen of Hearts under one arm. I carried the candy bags and Gus kept his other arm around my shoulder. I liked the way it felt. I tried not to think about the short boy, but snips of his words kept floating into my mind.

Gus's arm was comforting. If anyone walked past us, they'd think we were on a date. That boy had thought I was Gus's girlfriend, too. Even though he'd scared me, remembering his words excited me, too. No one had ever spoken to me like that before.

Back at our house, the pumpkins in the hall windows were dark. The candles had burned out and the features drooped, caving inward, old and sad. I wiped my face one more time before going in.

8

Gus and I didn't mention Halloween to each other. I didn't tell anybody else about it, either. For a few days it didn't bother me. Then I remembered little things, like the look in the shortest boy's eye and the way I'd shivered when he reached for my costume. I decided to talk to my mother.

On Emma's day off, Mom and I walked to the North End to buy vegetables. She liked the open markets and cafés. "The tomatoes aren't wrapped in cellophane," she said. She took her sisal basket and two string bags. "Let's pretend we're in Europe." We always stopped first at a café for coffee and pastry. Then we walked along the narrow streets looking over the mounds of vegetables and fruit—eggplants, strawberries, green and red peppers—and the fish, laid out in rows on chips of ice, smelling tangy.

Mom bought two types of food: things we always used, like tomatoes and green peppers, lettuce, bananas, and peaches; and things she was curious about or thought looked pretty, like endive, rutabaga, or pomegranates. The second type made Emma sigh and bang pots around in the drawers. "What am I supposed to do with this, I'd like to know?" she'd say, holding up a coconut, or some kale.

We found a window table at Café Luna. Mom fluffed her hair out with both hands and smoothed the little wrinkle between her eyebrows. She thought it gave her age away and whenever she remembered, she smoothed it flat. In her jeans and striped sweater, she looked like a tall skinny kid to me, except for her few gray hairs. As she read the menu, I traced the veins in the marble tabletop, not sure how to start.

"You were right about my Halloween costume," I said. "It was too short. I should've worn jeans."

"Too cold?"

"No. Remember, you were worried that something might happen? You were right."

Mom put the menu down.

"I didn't want to tell you but it keeps bothering me."

"Why didn't you want to tell me?"

"I was afraid you'd never let me go out again." I tried to make it sound like a joke. "I guess we stayed out too long. Halloween changes if you stay out late." I told her about the three boys, their boots and jackets, the things they said. She listened, stirring her cappuccino with a little spoon. When I got to the part about my costume ripping, she shook her head. I told her how we'd run home, but not about Gus giving me his jacket.

When I finished, she sat for a few seconds tapping the table with her spoon. I was afraid she was mad at me until she reached over and held my hand in both of hers. I started to cry. I covered my face with my hands but the tears leaked out and made dark spots on the red paper place mat.

"I'm glad you told me, Miranda, and I'm glad you weren't hurt. What kind of world is this when kids can't go trick-or-treating?"

Mom gave me her hanky with the blue flowers around the edge. I wiped my eyes. "You were lucky, you could have met rougher customers. I hate to think of it."

"Do you think it's my fault because I wore that costume? Emma says it's a woman's fault. Maybe if I'd worn jeans, it wouldn't have happened."

"And maybe it would have. No, it's not your fault. You were minding your own business. That's an old line about it being the woman's fault. Emma told you that?"

I didn't want to get Emma in trouble but I'd already said it.

"What else did she tell you?" The nerve below Mom's left eye was twitching the way it does when she's tired or angry. "It's important, Miranda. What did she tell you?"

As I was talking, Mom propped her chin on her fist. She raised her eyebrows a few times, and when I said men couldn't control themselves, she groaned.

"When did Emma tell you all this?"

"Last week. She saw a chart I was drawing for Hygiene, and she talked to me."

"She sure did."

"Emma said sex hurts if you're the woman. Is that true?"

Mom let her breath out in a low whistle. "Emma said it hurts? She covered all the bases, didn't she?"

She stared out the window for a few minutes and shook her head as if she were talking to herself.

"When Emma was young, people didn't talk much about sex, and probably some women were frightened by it. They didn't understand their bodies, and they were ashamed to tell their partners how they felt or what they needed. I think that's what Emma meant. But it doesn't have to be like that." She smiled. "Making love should be comfortable, not painful. People like it, men and women both."

Mom motioned for me to finish my cocoa. "I hadn't realized how grown-up you're getting."

That made me smile.

Two days later Mom and Emma had a fight. It started as a private discussion.

"I know you've got plenty of homework," Mom said to me. "Close your door so we don't disturb you."

I can't remember ever being told to do that before. I sat on my bed for a while. Then I tried reading *Great Expec-*

tations for Rathbone's class. But I couldn't keep my mind on Pip. I cracked the door just enough to hear their voices, and listened with my face against the doorframe.

My mother's voice was low and angry. "The point is not whether she's ready, Emma. The question is who should tell her. A mother should tell her daughter those things—it's a mother's right!"

"A mother's right? I've raised that child since she was a baby. That has rights, too. It was time! A girl has to be told. If I'd waited for you to do it, she'd have been in college! You're hardly home for dinner half the time."

"What are you saying? That I don't take time for Miranda? How dare you say that! I give her every free minute I can squeeze and you know it."

"You're a busy woman, that's no secret. In my day women weren't doctors and lawyers. Now everything's changed. But children are children and somebody's got to raise them."

My mother didn't answer for a few moments. I could imagine her sitting at the table with her arms crossed, the angry nerve jumping in her cheek and the worry line a deep furrow. "I didn't realize you disapproved of my work and the way I raise my daughter."

Emma was talking fast the way she always did when she was upset. "I spoke to Miranda because I know it was the right thing to do. Now you're on your high horse about your place, my place. If I'm not wanted here, I'm happy to leave."

Emma leave? Her sister Ruth wanted her to come and

live in Florida, but Emma always said Ruth's apartment complex was full of lonely old women who sat by the pool all day pecking at each other like hens in a barnyard. If Emma left, who would take care of me?

My mother waited before she spoke. I heard Emma blow her nose twice. I hoped she wasn't crying. If Mom made Emma go, I'd never forgive her. At least she could ask me. I was the one Emma took care of.

"Emma, come on! We're not talking about your leaving. We're talking about what you said to Miranda. I hadn't realized how far apart we are in the ways we think. So much of what you told her I disagree with, profoundly. The things you said about not bathing or washing your hair when you have your period are just a lot of superstition. Old wives' tales. Women haven't believed that stuff in years! And calling it 'the curse'! Emma, that just frightens girls. It doesn't help them adjust. But what upset me the most is you told her that intercourse was painful, and all that baloney about men losing control and women having to shoulder all the responsibility for that, worrying about their clothes and how they sit and what they say. Why should the woman be the one who worries? I really object to you telling Miranda those dark old tales."

"You object? Tales, you call them? That doesn't surprise me. I know you think differently, Miss High and Mighty Lawyer. I can see that from the number of men you've carried on with."

"Carried on? I've had relationships, Emma. There's nothing wrong with that."

"A different man every year. What kind of model is that for a child?"

There was more silence. Then the telephone rang. It was for Mom. She hung up quickly.

Then Emma said, "I think it's best if I give my notice, Frances. I don't take well to being put in my place. I've always done what I thought was best for Miranda, but it seems as if that isn't good enough. You are her mother. I won't argue with that. Here's two weeks notice, then. I'll tell Miranda myself in the morning."

My mother cleared her throat. "I hadn't meant to end it like this, Emma. But if my work and my relationships offend you, I don't know what to say."

"You hadn't meant it? You come in and tell me that everything I've said is untrue, and you think I'd stay? Isn't that just like you, thinking you can tell me what to think and I won't mind. I have my pride. You're not the only one, you know."

That was the last I heard. A door closed. Emma must have gone to her room. My mother stayed in the kitchen by herself. My cheek hurt from pressing against the doorframe and my feet were cold. I changed into my nightgown, brushed my teeth, and got into bed. I almost never pray but Emma prayed every night so I said a prayer that she wouldn't really leave. Not until I went to college, please.

9

Emma called her sister, then reserved a sleeper berth on the train to Florida. When I tried to talk to her about it, she wouldn't say anything except, "Ask your mother."

I couldn't believe she was leaving. I couldn't imagine getting ready for the dance without her. Who would take me shopping for my dress? What about Thanksgiving? Who would buy the turkey? How do you cook turkey, anyway? When I knew Emma was leaving for sure, when she told me herself and I couldn't talk her out of it, I got mad at Mom. She was lying on the couch with her legs crossed, reading a new book from her Mystery Readers

Club, as if nothing was wrong, nothing had changed, as if there was no problem to solve right here in her own house. I sat on the coffee table, as close as I could get to her face.

"Why did you yell at Emma?" I said.

"I didn't yell," Mom said. She lay the book upside down on her stomach and sat up.

"Yes, you did. I heard you arguing."

"We argued, but we didn't yell."

"What's the difference? You made her leave."

"No, sweetheart, I did not make Emma leave. We both decided it was the best thing. It wasn't only my idea."

"You aren't stopping her."

"How can I stop her? She's sixty-one years old. She can do what she wants to do."

"You could apologize, say you were wrong."

"I could if I felt that way, but I don't."

"You should. You've ruined everything. You don't care what I think about this. She isn't your friend. You're never home."

"I know you're upset about this, Miranda." Mom spoke in that slow, patient voice she used when I was unreasonable or hysterical. "Emma's been part of our lives for a long time. But she and I have different opinions. That's all there is to it. She has old-fashioned views about sex and women. She shouldn't have told you what she did."

"But it didn't do any harm, Mom. You don't think I listened to that stuff about not washing my hair, do you?"

"Sweetheart, who knows what you listened to? I'm trying to raise you now, not fifty years ago. Things have changed and Emma has to realize it."

80

I hated to cry during an argument but I couldn't imagine living without Emma. I'd even miss the way we argued about my hair in my eyes, and about my setting the table or washing the dishes. I'd miss her when I came home from school. I'd miss her in the morning reminding me to pack my homework and brush my teeth.

Emma wouldn't let me stay home from school to see her off. "We can say good-bye in the morning," she told me. "I'll make a special breakfast. French toast, pancakes, or waffles? Bacon or sausage?"

My mother left early for the office to give me and Emma some time alone. I didn't feel like eating.

"Let's have a smile, Miranda. This isn't the end of the world. We can write to each other and talk on the phone."

"It won't be the same," I said.

"Of course it won't. Nothing stays the same forever, child. Look at you. You're big enough to watch out for yourself after school. You don't need me. You and your mother will get along fine."

"No, we won't."

"That's enough of that talk. There's a package for you to open. Something to help you remember me."

She handed me a little box wrapped in blue paper. I opened it and took out a statue of a little girl holding a star in one hand.

"It's a music box," Emma said. "It plays 'When You Wish Upon a Star.'"

I turned the key in the bottom and listened to the tinny notes. The statue was babyish. Four years ago I would have loved it, just the way I used to love the ballerina that

81

pirouetted on top of my jewelry box. Now I wondered where to put it. The song ended and I wound it up again. "Thank you, Emma."

"You can think of me when you listen to it," she said with an unsuspecting smile. "Hurry up now and eat before I have to call Gus to come down and finish this."

I hugged Emma good-bye when my bus came. "I'll miss you so much," I told her, crying into her shoulder. Her sweater smelled like the dusting powder she always used. It came in an oval box with roses on top and I bought it for her every birthday. Emma was crying, too. We hugged each other again and the bus blew its horn a second time.

"Run down there, now, before he pulls away. And be a good girl. I'll be thinking of you." Then she yelled out the window, "Coming!" I could see her waving from my seat on the bus.

When I came home from school that afternoon, the apartment was silent. I was supposed to go upstairs to the Llewellyns' until Mom got home. She'd arranged to be home at five. But I didn't go right upstairs. I took off my backpack and sat on my bed. It was so quiet. I hadn't often been in the apartment alone, without Emma or my mother there. I could hear the old clock ticking in the living room, and the hum of the refrigerator. I walked through the rooms touching things, the photos on the mantel, the carved wooden fruit in the bowl on the coffee table, the lion paperweight from my grandfather's desk. I walked slowly into Emma's room, half hoping it was unchanged.

The room still had furniture—the bed, the bureau, the little armchair, the desk. The curtains with the climbing roses hung at the windows. The matching spread lay folded at the foot of the mattress. A rose-colored rug covered most of the floor. Rose was Emma's favorite color. She'd vacuumed and dusted, but left the bed to air. Every surface was blank, stripped bare. How often had I come in here in the middle of the night, after a dream, or when I was lonely in my bed? How often had I snuggled under Emma's afghan and watched her put her curlers in?

"Miranda, are you home?" Carol called. I heard her cross the living room, the dining room, and come down the hall looking for me. When she saw me standing in Emma's room, she hugged me and we stood in the middle of the rug, swaying back and forth a little, as if I was a baby and she was rocking me. I didn't pull away.

I went upstairs with Carol after that. Gus and I worked on *Alien Attraction* for a while and I played two games of Candyland with Sebastian. From four-thirty on, I kept checking downstairs to see if Mom was home yet. I looked in our refrigerator but I couldn't see anything for dinner except eggs. I hated eating eggs at night. If you're going to eat eggs, why not eat cereal or toast? How can anyone sleep after a dinner like that? Your stomach would growl so loud you'd wake up.

I sat in the Llewellyns' kitchen watching Carol chop onions for stew. Gus was upstairs listening to his tape of "The War of the Worlds." Orson Welles's deep voice announced that the Martians had landed. Gus was saying the lines along with Welles. I could see why people believed it was a real newscast when they first heard it on the radio. In the living room, Sebastian was building a castle for his

knights and singing his current favorite song, "La Bamba."
I didn't get the Spanish words right so he sang extra loud
to make up.

I was helping Carol peel carrots when I heard my mother
whistle. I left the peeler on the counter and ran downstairs.
She was unpacking a bag of groceries onto the counter.

"Hi, sweets. Spaghetti with sausage, hamburgers, or tuna
salad?"

"Hamburgers," I said. "With french fries."

"Let's not be too ambitious on the first day. How about
baked potatoes and frozen peas? I think we can handle
that."

I scrubbed the potatoes, pricked them with a fork, and
put them in the oven. Mom made the hamburgers but she
didn't put in any seasoning. Emma made them with horse-
radish, garlic, and Worcestershire sauce.

"How was school?" Mom asked. She put the hamburgers in the frying pan and turned the burner on. "Is everybody excited about the dance?" The skillet was beginning
to smoke.

"Mom, I think you better turn the flame down under
the hamburgers."

"If you sear the outside, it keeps the juices in." She turned
on the fan above the stove and flipped the hamburgers
over. Drops of grease splattered, the flames jutted up
around the sides of the pan, and then the inside of the pan
started to flame, too. "Hand me the salt, quick!" Mom
said. She turned off the burner and poured salt on the fire.
The flames disappeared. The hamburgers were charred

lumps, covered with salt. I wanted to laugh and cry. Would every dinner be like this?

"How about pizza?" Mom said. We phoned in our order and walked over to pick it up. It was a nice treat, but if all our meals turned out like this one we'd starve. Maybe Carol could give me cooking lessons.

While we were eating I remembered the dance. "I've got to get a dress for the dance."

"When's the dance?"

"The weekend before Thanksgiving. Which reminds me, what'll we do for Thanksgiving?" If Mom couldn't cook hamburgers, how could she ever manage a turkey?

"Without Emma, you mean? I thought we'd go to McDonald's and have a couple of Big Macs or a box of Chicken McNuggets. The chicken would be more festive. Closer to turkey. Unless you want a Happy Meal."

"Mom, come on, what're we going to do?"

"Lucia called me at work and invited us for the weekend. Grandma told her about Emma leaving, and she was worried about us. Everybody thinks I'm incompetent."

"Aunt Lucia's? Will Ray and Tina be home?"

"Yes, everyone's back on the East Coast this year, so Lucia's staging a big family Thanksgiving. They're all anxious to see you. Tina's living right here in Boston, taking acting lessons and living in a dump near the university. I'm going to call and offer her a ride."

That settled Thanksgiving. The dance was still a problem. Mom said she'd take me shopping on Saturday but I hadn't invited Gus yet. Thursday, on the way home from school, listening to two of the Cynthias in the seat behind me giggling about the dance, I got an idea. When we worked on *Alien Attraction*, I'd have Teresa invite Vortrum, and that would give Gus the idea, and then I'd invite Gus for real.

Gus and I sat on his window seat as usual. Now that daylight saving time had ended, it started to get dark after four-thirty. Gus dragged over the standing lamp from his worktable. I wrapped a quilt around my legs to keep warm.

"I've got an idea," I said. "Teresa's met Vortrum, and she wants to invite him somewhere."

"Where?" Gus asked.

"Let me write the beginning of the scene, then I'll give it to you and you'll be surprised. Your answer will sound better that way." I didn't want him to say no right away, before I'd written anything.

I began writing. Usually it's hard for me to start, but not this time.

> Teresa wanted to see Vortrum, the alien, again. She wanted to let him know he was her friend and he could trust her. He said he wanted to know everything about Earth, and about teenagers. I'll ask him to the Junior Dance, she thought. We'll have a chance to talk, and he can see one of the things that teenagers do together.
>
> She walked to the park and sat on the bench where she'd first met Vortrum, when she was baby-sitting. She sat on the bench and waited, hoping he'd appear again. She began to feel silly sitting there by herself

*on a cloudy fall day. Just when she was about to go
home, she saw him walking down the path. He was
still wearing his space boots, but this time he had on
blue jeans and a sweatshirt with them.*

*He grinned and waved when he saw her, then hur-
ried to the bench and sat beside her.*

"You came back," he said.

*"That's what I was going to say to you," said Ter-
esa. "I wanted to ask you something, Vortrum. Would
you come with me to a dance at my school?"*

I read the beginning again, and handed the notebook to
Gus. He read it with a smile until he got to the last line.
"A dance?"

I nodded.

"Why would they do that?"

"That's what teenagers do," I said.

"Maybe in your romance novels, but not in real life. We
don't go to dances, do we?"

"Because we haven't been old enough."

"Because we're smart enough to know how dumb they
are. How can we write about a dance if we've never been
to one?"

Sometimes a plan goes exactly as you hoped. "There's
a dance at Miss Ayers next week and I have to go. You
can come with me. We'll do research and then we can write
the dance chapter and it'll be funny. Please, Gus! Come
with me?"

"I can't dance," Gus said.

"I'll teach you. It's easy."

"I don't want to learn to dance."

"Please, Gus. If you go as Vortrum, you can pretend you've never seen anything like it, and you'll have all these strange ideas about what's going on. It'll be funny."

"Why do you have to go?"

"Mom says it's good experience. Everybody in my class is going. The boys are from other schools, but we can bring a guest if we like."

"What do I have to wear? If it's a suit, I'm definitely not coming."

"No suit." I knew he'd come. Good old Vortrum.

Now that I knew Gus was coming to the dance, I even enjoyed dance class a little the next Friday. Miss Leopold, in bright red this time, acted as if she were going to the dance.

"So who's found a dress?" she asked.

Cynthia One raised her hand. "It's white on top with a pink skirt," she said, smiling at her friends.

"Oooh," said Miss Leopold, "that sounds lovely, like Cinderella at the ball."

"I'm going to throw up," said Catherine in my ear.

"How fancy a dress does it have to be?" Morna asked.

"Think of it this way, girls, a dance dress is a dream dress," Miss Leopold fluttered her scarf.

"Now I am really going to puke. She wants us to look like Barbie at the prom. Don't you wish you didn't have to go?" Catherine asked.

"Gus is coming with me. He's pretending he's Vortrum going to his first dance on Earth."

"Gus is coming? How'd you talk him into it?"

"I said we could pretend to be Vortrum and Teresa. He said okay."

"I can't believe it. He's not the dance type. Maybe I'll come, too. I have a cousin I could drag along. Dennis could keep Gus company."

She acted as if she knew all about Gus, and it bothered me. He was my best friend, not hers, and he wasn't a type.

Miss Leopold started the records and we practiced the box step, the fox trot, and the waltz. Twice I landed on Catherine's foot. I didn't mean to. The second time, she hopped around holding her foot in her hand. Miss Leopold stopped the record player.

"Girls, be careful! Imagine, Miranda, if that had happened at the dance, how embarrassed you would have been, and your poor escort!"

"Escort? What about me?" Catherine said.

It couldn't have hurt that much. If she'd stepped on my foot, I wouldn't have made a fuss. I was so angry at her that I thought of stepping on the same foot again, on purpose.

"Say hi to Gus for me," Catherine said later when we were waiting for the bus. I nodded, but I forgot when I got home.

I'd been shopping with my mother before, but never for a dress to wear to a dance.

"Let's try downtown first, and if we don't find anything, we'll try Harvard Square."

"Harvard Square? Why would we go there?"

"You're not the frilly type, and usually the department stores have a lot of satin and velvet this time of year. They must think we're all performing in *The Nutcracker*."

At Jordan's, Mom showed me a green velvet dress with a full skirt, lace collar, and pink satin sash. "This is almost exactly like a dress my mother made me wear for my piano recital when I was fourteen. I felt like some gigantic baby up in front of everyone."

Mom put the dress back on the rack. "You should always feel like yourself," she said. "It's important to find your own style. When you find clothes that make you comfortable, you'll have a better time, because you go as yourself, not somebody else."

I thought about the boring lawyer suits she wore to work. They didn't look comfortable. Maybe she was just talking about weekends or after work.

I told Mom what Miss Leopold said about dance dresses being dream dresses. Mom just shook her head. "I can't wait to meet this woman. When I drive you to the dance, I'll sneak in and get a look."

"But don't stay."

We didn't find anything downtown so Mom took me to the Square. In the first store, everything was black and lime green, and the salesgirls had jewels in their noses. In the next store, Mom spotted a skinny black jumper with a scooped front and a big kick pleat in back. She had me try it on over a silky red shirt with wide sleeves that ended in a cuff below my elbows.

"You look like a Spanish dancer without the ruffles."

We found red flats at the shoe store next door, and Mom bought me black net stockings. "Do it right," she said.

When I got home, I put everything on together and looked in the mirror. I felt as sleek as a cat.

"Let's try a French braid," Mom said. She brushed my hair back, and caught the sides in the braid, pulling up as she wove the strands down the center of my head. She even put makeup lightly on my eyes and lips.

"Hoop earrings, I think, and lots of bracelets." When she was all through she said, "Let's sneak Carol down and get her opinion."

"Just Carol. Nobody else," I said.

Carol and Mom made me model in the living room. As I walked back and forth between the desk and the piano, I remembered parading for Mom and Emma on Halloween, and wondered what Emma would think of my outfit. She liked velvet and satin dresses, and lace collars, too.

"Terrific!" said Carol. "Just right. Not too fancy but very fancy, if you know what I mean. The blouse is great! What can I lend you? An evening bag? I've got a little black one with a gold chain. How about bracelets?"

"Do you have any bangles?" Mom asked. "I've got two, but it would look great to have a few on each arm with those sleeves. What do you think, Miranda?"

When Emma and Mom used to discuss me, they left me out, as if I was too young to have an opinion. But this time, I felt included, part of a team. I was excited about the dance. Me, excited about the dance!

10

The first week after Emma left, the house stayed clean enough. The dirt needed time to accumulate before it showed. But Mom wasn't satisfied. She tried doing the laundry and housework when she came home from work and she nagged about everything. She complained that I left grease on the serving bowl and the pots weren't clean. I'd never even washed the pots and pans before. I told her I used hot water but she said, "Not hot enough." She hounded me to pick up the towels on the bathroom floor, put away the peanut butter, and take out the trash.

"Why do I have to take it out? It smells." I hated the

back alley where we kept the garbage cans. Once I'd seen a dead rat back there. Emma almost never made me take out the garbage.

"It's you or me, toots, and I did it Tuesday. Pickup's tomorrow, so we have to get it out tonight," Mom shouted over the noise of the vacuum.

"I never had to do it when Emma was here."

"Emma treated you like a princess. New regime!" The way she laughed, it sounded as if she was happy about the change.

"I hate this. I wish Emma was back. If you hadn't been so mean to her, she wouldn't have left."

Mom clicked the vacuum off with her toe and wiped her forehead. "You hate this? I love it, Miranda. I love it. I love working all day and coming home to this pigsty." She was shouting. I hoped the Llewellyns wouldn't hear her. "I love it so much I think I'll stop right now." She kicked the vacuum on its side. Then she left, just like that. At six o'clock on Thursday night, without making dinner or saying good-bye. She grabbed her jacket from its hook in the hall closet, picked up her keys and pocketbook and walked out.

I waited for a few minutes but she didn't come back. I took out the trash, two bags of it. I even emptied the wastepaper basket in the bathroom. I put the vacuum cleaner back in the hall closet. Then I took a container of peach yogurt out of the refrigerator and ate it in the living room, watching a show about gorilla babies on TV. Mom came back at seven-forty. Her eyes were red.

I turned off the TV.

She walked into the kitchen, took out a can of tomato soup and a can opener and began to open the lid. "Want some?" she asked.

She didn't mention where she'd been. I didn't ask. It was a truce. Neither of us said anything about housework, dirt, or garbage for a few careful days. The next Monday night, I took out the trash without being asked. In my whole life, I had never seen my mother explode like that.

The week before the dance, I tried to teach Gus some steps. Carol found us records to practice to. Gus insisted on wearing his father's hat. "Like Fred Astaire," he said. He crossed his legs and spun around. If there'd been a cane in the house, he would have twirled it.

I tried to show him the basics. "Just count the beats. It's simple."

"Let's improvise," he said. He shuffled a few steps, turned around, dipped to one side, shuffled some more, leaving me standing alone in the middle of the living room.

"I can't follow you when you improvise." I didn't want to criticize too much because I was afraid he'd back out and I'd be stuck going alone.

Carol rescued me. "Augustus, stop pretending you know what you're doing and learn these steps so you won't embarrass all of us." She made him dance with her, and she counted like a drill sergeant. By the end of the week, he only improvised on the cha-cha, and I didn't care. He kept the count, so we could stay sort of together.

"You get to pick the pizza, Gus," I told him. It was my

way of saying thanks for going. He chose pepperoni, sausage, green pepper, and onions.

"You better chew mints on the way to the dance," Mom said when she called in the order. "You could decimate a partner with your breath after eating that."

After supper Mom braided my hair and put some makeup on me. "What do you think?" she asked, turning me around to face the mirror. It was me, but not so pale. My eyes looked bigger. With my hair up, my face wasn't so much like a full moon rising. I put on her big gold hoop earrings and slipped three bangle bracelets on each arm.

Gus came down with his hair combed slightly flatter than usual. He had on a blue shirt, his father's tweed jacket, and his own corduroy pants.

"Like my tie?" he asked. It was red paisley. The design looked like bugs. "I found it at The Albatross. I was looking for a cane, but had to settle for this."

Thank goodness he hadn't found a cane. Miss Leopold might think it was a weapon.

Mom drove us to school and parked the car in the circle. I led the way to the auditorium.

"Remember, Mom, you promised not to stay."

"I just want to peek at Miss Leopold and see the dresses, then I'll vanish. I'll pick you up at ten out front."

Miss Leopold stood at the door, glittering like a Christmas tree ornament in a filmy white dress and silver shoes. Even her eyelids sparkled. When she held out her hand to my mother, her nails were silver, too.

I introduced my mother and Gus.

"Delighted," Miss Leopold gushed.

I pushed Gus through the door before she could add any more baloney. Mom whispered, "That outfit must have come from Central Casting. Miss Haversham, that's who she is."

"Miss Haversham's a crazy old lady in *Great Expectations* who's waiting forever for her fiancé," I told Gus. "He jilted her before the wedding but she keeps on waiting."

The girls huddled on the left side of the room, whispering in groups while the boys milled around on the right. The decoration committee had strung white and silver streamers from the overhead lights, with tiny white lights woven in and out. It looked almost snowy.

"Have fun, chickens. See you later," Mom said.

I stood with Gus, feeling shy. I'd never been to a dance before. I didn't know what to do with him.

I spotted Miss Rathbone wearing an embroidered purple dress that looked like it came from an exotic country. Maybe she traveled in the summers. She even had on purple shoes, but her gray hair and glasses were the same. She smiled and waved. I waved back.

"Want to meet Rathbone?" I asked Gus. We walked over to the doorway, weaving in between the people who were just arriving.

"Miss Rathbone, this is my friend Gus."

"I thought so. Gus, I recognized you from the portrait Miranda wrote. You're a writer yourself, aren't you?" Miss Rathbone said.

Gus nodded, pleased by the description.

"Have fun tonight," she said.

We walked toward the front of the room. "Let's see if there's anything to eat," Gus said. We circled around but spotted nothing. We were heading for chairs in the corner when Miss Leopold fluttered into the middle of the room and clapped her hands.

"Welcome to the first of the Junior Dances, boys and girls. We're so happy to see you here tonight in our Winter Wonderland. We'll introduce you to your partner and then we'll start the music. Boys, line up by height on the right. And girls on the left, the shortest in front. Those of you who came with a partner don't need to join the line."

The pairing-off moved quickly. The boys clowned and pushed each other in their line. The girls whispered or stared straight ahead with arms crossed, as if walking toward the noose. Tiny Millie was third in line and Louise was almost last. They both looked nervous. Millie was biting her lip. I glanced at Gus. He was studying the lights.

"Too bad they didn't use the ones that turn on and off," he said. "They could have made icicles, too. How could they do snow? Maybe styrofoam, some sort of recycle system so it would get sucked up off the floor and blown out up at the ceiling again."

"Hi!" Catherine sneaked up behind us. "I decided to come after all. My cousin Dennis said he didn't mind coming, right, Dennis?"

Dennis was shorter than Catherine. His braces looked as if they hurt the inside of his lips.

"Boys and girls," Miss Leopold called from the front

of the room. "The first dance will be a box step."

Gus and I moved to the edge of the dance floor and got in position, my hand on Gus's shoulder, his hand on my waist, my right hand in his left. It felt silly standing there before the music started. Gus made a face with his eyebrows up and his mouth down, like Stan Laurel. Then the record started: "Winter Wonderland."

I heard Catherine groan, "Corny!" If she'd been two inches taller, she could rest her chin on top of Dennis's head. I waved to her with my left hand. She winked. Her dress was sea blue, and made her eyes look even bluer than usual. She'd pulled her hair back so it curled around the ribbon in a crown shape.

I could hear Gus counting under his breath. He smelled spicy from his father's after-shave. His hand pressed my back lightly. I wondered if my hand was sweaty, the one he was holding. I hoped not. I couldn't do anything about it anyway. I didn't step on his feet, and he didn't step on mine. I tried hard to follow without tripping and I sang along with the song. I knew the words because Mom always sang it when we went walking in the snow. The box step was monotonous. We stayed in the same place because we didn't know how to move around, but a few couples managed to circle the floor. "Let's try to move," Gus said. "Every time we count one, we'll shift over."

I looked at his feet and tried to follow. We lurched up the side of the room and then across the front by the stage. Miss Leopold gave me an enthusiastic smile and mouthed the word, "Wonderful," with her eyes open wide like a fish.

"Like driving a truck through traffic," Gus said.

"I'm the truck?"

"No, you're okay. But I have to steer us around, you know?"

The next dance was a waltz. As soon as we managed to bob at the same time, Gus started moving again. This time, he didn't stay at the edge of the group, but dodged between pairs of dancers instead.

"Close call," he muttered. "Watch out on the right. Coming through."

It was more like a bumper car ride than a waltz. We got dirty looks and elbows and one of the Cynthias, wearing pink, of course, kicked my ankle, on purpose, I think.

"Let's sit down," I said at the end of the song.

We sat next to a rubber plant. Catherine saw us and sat down, too. Dennis grinned but still didn't say anything. He was the silent type.

"Your hair looks great. Who did it?" Catherine asked.

"My mom. She lent me these earrings, too."

"My mom wouldn't know how to start doing a braid like that. She wanted me to wear gloves. How do you like that?"

Catherine sounded different than usual. Why was she talking about clothes and hair? She didn't even laugh when I pointed out three Cynthias in pink dresses standing together by the mirror.

"Come to the bathroom with me?" she asked.

"Be right back," I told Gus. He was cracking his knuckles.

After the dim auditorium, the hall lights glared. The bathroom was crowded with girls fixing their hair and peering at themselves in the mirror to see if anything had smudged. We pushed to the front and I washed my hands while Catherine put water on her eyebrows.

"They're too bushy," she said. "Do me a favor?"

"Sure."

"Make Gus dance with me a few times? You can dance with Dennis."

"I don't know."

"Why not?"

"Maybe he'll think I'm trying to get rid of him or something. I don't want to hurt his feelings."

"Don't be a jerk. How would it hurt his feelings? You're being selfish."

"Selfish?"

"You just want to keep him to yourself, and I'm stuck with my cousin."

"He's my best friend."

"But he's not your boyfriend."

"So what?"

"So maybe he'd get to like me."

She made it sound like a contest. "If you want to dance with him, ask him yourself," I said.

"Okay, I will."

She shoved her way back to the door. "Hey, watch it," someone said.

Gus and Dennis had found some punch and cookies and they were playing cards with Dennis's deck. Catherine and

all the fast dancing, it felt good to just move in small steps, leaning on each other a little. Gus put his cheek against my hair, tilting his head. I hoped the song was long, it felt so good to drift like this, so close together. When the song finally ended, the big overhead lamps came on, and we moved apart slowly, blinking like moles.

When we climbed into the backseat together, Mom asked, "How was it?"

"Not bad," said Gus. "Nobody laughed."

"Mom, Gus can really dance. We even moved around." I jabbed him gently in the side.

"Maybe by the next one we can learn to tap dance. That would shock 'em," Gus said.

Too tired to answer, I sank down in the seat and let my head lean against the sleeve of his coat.

11

My Aunt Lucia's house was built of fieldstone two hundred years ago. The first time I went there, my father was still alive. I don't remember it, but my mother has a picture of me sitting on the front step beside my aunt's spaniel. I'm wearing a knit hat with a pom-pom, and the puppy is licking my cheek. There's a shadow beside me on the step from the person taking the picture. I think it's my father.

We drove up to Lucia's Wednesday afternoon. Mom picked me up at Miss Ayers. I changed into jeans in the school bathroom as soon as my last class was dismissed:

no way would I wear my uniform to Aunt Lucia's. My cousin Tina sat in the front seat. I climbed in back.

"I can't believe how big you are," Tina said. "I haven't seen you in at least two years, right? I didn't get home much when I was in college."

Tina looked different, too. Her hair was long, below her shoulders.

"I hope we beat the traffic," Mom said. "Thanksgiving is the worst. But this gives us a chance to talk. How many of you live in that apartment?"

"It was supposed to be just me and these two guys I knew from college," Tina said. "But they decided that the rent was too steep. They're musicians, and they never have enough money. They need to keep time open in case their group gets bookings, but they also have to earn enough to live on. That's a problem. They decided to let two other guys from the group move in and share their rooms. Now it's me and the four of them, a trumpet player, a sax, a bass player, and the drummer. High Spirits Jazz Quartet, living right in my apartment. I have to go to work in the morning but they're up till two or three A.M. and sleep until noon. Snow White and the four musicians. They never clean, they don't even wash their own dishes. I'm going crazy."

My mother laughed. "It sounds like a situation comedy. Not funny when it's happening to you, I'm sure. Can't you do something about it?"

"I'm looking around. Something will open up. It's got to. Yesterday, I had to take the drummer's dirty socks off the kitchen table before I could eat breakfast. I thought my brother was a slob, but Ray's nothing compared to High Spirits. You know what the worst of it is? My friends say, 'You live with High Spirits? They're so cute.' Cute? You don't care what your roommates look like when you're living with them. I don't think they're cute. I think they're pigs."

"You better get out of there fast, Tina," Mom said.

"At least it gives me material for my improvisation class. Last week I did a piece about a woman who's tired of picking up after her family. Mr. Morse, my acting teacher, liked it, and he never gives compliments."

After a while, I got tired of trying to listen to their front-seat conversation so I balled up my sweater against the window as a pillow, pulled the car blanket over me and went to sleep. Mom woke me when we pulled into the driveway at Aunt Lucia's.

The spaniel came out to greet us. His tail wagged but his legs were so stiff that he could only walk slowly toward the car. His muzzle was gray.

"Remy, you sweet old guy," Tina said, stooping down to rub his head.

Aunt Lucia followed behind him, the front of her jeans and sweater covered with flour. "We match," she said pointing to Remy's muzzle. She hugged my mother. "Excuse my mess, Franny. It's so good to see you! And Miranda, look at you. I can't believe it. Come and give your old aunt a kiss."

Aunt Lucia wasn't old, but her hair was gray. She wore

it cut almost as short as a man's, and her face was tan from gardening. She grew a lot of vegetables and had pear trees and apple trees, grapevines and even three beehives. She worked as a medical illustrator, with her studio in the barn.

"Ray's getting in late tonight. He's bringing his current friend, Helene. I won't say any more." She picked up Mom's suitcase and led the way to the house.

Tina explained. "She thinks Helene's a spoiled little whiner, and hopes Ray won't get snagged into marrying her. Nobody's good enough for your little boy, huh, Mom?"

"Don't tease. I'm trying to be good. Helene's Ray's friend."

"She wears heavy makeup and high-heeled boots," Tina added. "Don't worry, Mom. Ray knows what he's doing."

"See what headaches they give me, Fran. Be happy Miranda's still young." Lucia led us into the kitchen. The table and the floor around it were covered with flour. "Pie crusts," she explained. "Franny, your room is upstairs, the one with the little study. You can get away from all of us if you need to. You probably brought work. And Miranda, you're next door. If you like, you can get settled in and we still have time for a walk before it gets dark."

Mom and Lucia and I hiked to the top of the hill. The path was squishy with soggy leaves, and the air smelled of woodsmoke from chimneys. I walked along the top of an old wall part way up the hill, balancing on the uneven stones. Then I trailed behind them for a while, letting them talk. When Mom was just out of college, she and Lucia sang in a chorus together. Lucia asked Mom if she'd like to meet her younger brother, and that's how Mom and Dad met.

My mother had on her navy duffel with the hood and Lucia wore an old army jacket. As the sun went down, they faded more and more into the shadows, and I hurried to keep up.

Tina had a fire going in the living room when we got back. I sat in the corner working on the border of a jigsaw that Tina had put out. Mom and Aunt Lucia lay on the rug in front of the fireplace.

"Are you seeing anyone?" Lucia asked.

Mom shrugged. "Nobody special."

"But you're dating?"

Mom tossed little pieces of kindling twigs into the fire and watched them flare up.

"Anyone promising at least?" Lucia said. "Other lawyers? Guys from work?"

Mom shook her head. "Nobody, Lucia. I'm not seeing anyone. I haven't dated anyone since Jim last year. I'm ashamed to be such a recluse."

Lucia propped herself up on her elbows. "It's nothing to be ashamed of. They say a woman's more likely to be kidnapped by terrorists than she is to get married when she's over thirty-five."

"Is that supposed to make me feel better?"

"Suit yourself. You aren't even dating? Why not, for God's sake? You must get asked, don't you?"

"I'm too busy, especially now that Emma's gone." She rolled over on her back and crossed her arms under her head. "Just trying to keep up with the housework is killing me. Ask Miranda. I'm a crazy woman. Cooking, cleaning—it's too much. I need a wife. Who cares about men to date? I need a wife! I never knew how much Emma did."

"Why did she quit?" Lucia asked. "I thought she'd grow old with you two."

"We had a big fight."

"Over what?"

"Over sex."

"You're kidding."

"It's hard to explain," Mom said. "Emma gave Miranda an old-fashioned lecture filled with wives' tales, harmless maybe, but terrible stuff. I overreacted and she quit."

"So now what are you doing?"

"Coming home early. The Llewellyns are upstairs—Carol checks on Miranda after school. We can handle it, unless I get a case that involves travel. But for now, except for the housework, I like it this way. We have time to talk."

"Will you hire someone new?" Lucia asked.

"I don't know if we could get used to someone new at this point. Miranda's not a baby. Maybe a cleaning lady who comes once a week. A bossy housekeeper wouldn't fit us anymore, though it did for so long!"

"You'll work something out. Try frozen dinners. Do you have a microwave? But let's get back to the dating, Franny. You've got to be lonely, aren't you?"

"Maybe I've gotten used to it. I haven't met anyone I like, not since Daniel. I was just treading water with Jim. I don't want to do that again."

"Are you scared?"

"Scared of what?" Mom asked.

"Of trying it again? I don't know. Maybe you're afraid of losing someone again? Who am I to lecture? Married for twenty-six years, easy for me to give advice."

They both laughed. Then Mom stood up and stretched. "Let me help with dinner."

I took Mom's spot in front of the fire and watched the flames. I hoped I'd have a chance to ask Aunt Lucia about my father. I wanted to know what he was like when he was my age. Did he play any sports? Did he like to read? Did he get into trouble? Maybe she wouldn't remember, but at least I could ask.

After a while my face felt roasted, so I went into the kitchen. Just as we finished setting the table, Uncle Davis came home. "Hello, hello!" he said to us, kissing Mom and ruffling the top of my hair. "I should've left at noon. Remind me next year, will you, Lucy?" He kissed her and sat down.

"I bet Ray won't get here until after midnight," said Aunt Lucia. "I hope he drives safely."

"Maybe he'll let Helene drive," said Tina.

"She probably drives even faster than he does," Aunt Lucia said.

"I like that girl. She's got zip," said Uncle Davis.

"No taste," said Lucia.

"I married you," countered Uncle Davis. "I like women with style."

"You love to bait me." She shook her finger at him.

I didn't see Ray or Helene until after lunchtime on Thanksgiving, when they finally appeared and made themselves breakfast. Helene had on one of Ray's college sweatshirts and a pair of shiny black running tights. She had long curly hair that looked uncombed but she'd put on eye makeup and perfume. Ray stared at her as he drank his coffee.

When they'd finished, Aunt Lucia shooed them out of the kitchen and started dinner preparations. The turkey was already cooking. We could smell it all over the house. Mom and Tina were peeling and chopping vegetables.

"I've got a special job for you, Miranda. Would you make the centerpiece?" She gave me a bag of nuts, and one filled with different kinds of fruit—apples, pears, bananas, grapefruit, even a pineapple. "There are baskets in the pantry, candles in the drawer. Use whatever you like."

The table was already covered with a white cloth. I picked a wide, low basket, piled it full of fruit, and dotted the arrangement with nuts. I put burnt-orange candles in two candelabras and set one on each side. The cooks were still busy when I finished. Ray and Uncle Davis were watching football on TV in the den, and Helene sat on the couch next to Ray, painting her nails. I hated football, and the kitchen was crowded. So I whistled for Remy and went out for another walk. On the way home I gathered an armful of dried weeds, with pods and the remnants of old blossoms. I arranged them in another basket for the front-hall table. Then it was time to change.

"Dinner everyone," Aunt Lucia called.

Grandma Ruth, Uncle Davis's mother, had arrived while I was walking Remy. She brought chocolate turkeys for everyone, and set them at each place.

Uncle Davis said the grace, then carved the turkey and served everyone white meat, dark meat, or drumsticks. Ray wanted the neck! Serving dishes passed up and down the table—mashed potatoes, stuffing, green beans, candied yams, turnips, cranberry sauce, gravy with giblets, and hot rolls and butter. I worried that my plate might leak over the sides onto the tablecloth.

It was hard not to stare at Helene. Her nails were painted purple and she wore a black velvet dress with a low scooped neck. Helene's fork never stopped moving from her plate to her mouth and back as she mowed through the potatoes and turkey, and when Grandma Ruth asked her questions, she mumbled. A look of pain crossed Aunt Lucia's face.

By dessert, the dining room windows were dark. I could see our reflection, lit by the candles and the chandelier, bright against the night. A big family. It made me think about Mom and me, just the two of us. Such a tiny family. What if anything ever happened to one of us? Maybe Mom *should* get married again. Then we'd be three people at least, in case anything happened.

12

Ray and Helene left on Friday morning, Ray in his down vest and Helene in a raccoon coat. Ray kissed his mother quickly. He knew that she knew he was leaving early. When they waved from the car, both Ray and Helene looked relieved to be going, happy to escape Aunt Lucia's disapproval. Friday afternoon, Mom, Tina, Lucia, and I all went to an auction, and I didn't have a chance to ask Aunt Lucia any of my questions.

On the ride back home Saturday, the sky was gray and it snowed on Sunday, light flakes all day long, hardly enough to stick. All afternoon, Gus and I sat on his window seat and watched the flakes drift past, sometimes swirling in spirals, mostly just floating gently past the window. I leaned back against the cushions. The radiator in the corner hissed. I was coloring in the countries on a map of Africa and Gus was writing *Alien Attraction*. The tip of his tongue stuck out a little the way it does when he's concentrating.

"What're you writing?" I asked.

"Vortrum's seeing snow for the first time. He thinks it's poison sent by an enemy planet."

I colored in the sea around the continent. Catherine had shown me a new way to do it. She made short lines very close together around the whole coastline, blue and green, like fur sticking out. Then she wrapped a tissue around her finger and rubbed the border so it turned into a fuzzy band of color. She also outlined the countries in a dark band of a color, then colored the inside lightly in the same shade. When she rubbed it with a tissue, it blended together. Catherine's maps were so perfect they could be in a book. But she said it was too boring to study them, so she flunked the tests on the names and capitals every time.

Gus finished writing and handed me the notebook.

"The Menace of Snow," he'd written at the top of the page. He liked titles.

When Vortrum looked out the window in the morning, he gasped. "What's happening?" he wondered. The trees and grass had disappeared. Instead of brown and green, the world was white. More white stuff fell out of the sky. Nobody was outside. "They are all *hiding,"* he thought. *Quickly Vortrum dialed Teresa's number on the telephone. Her father answered in a sleepy voice. Vortrum asked for Teresa.*

"Do you know what time it is?" her father asked. "It's ten after six on Sunday morning."

"I need to speak to Teresa," Vortrum said. He didn't know people slept late on Sunday. He heard her father say something about crazy kids, and then Teresa came to the phone.

"The land is destroyed," he told her. "An enemy spaceship attacked during the night, spreading white poison over everything. More poison is falling still. It's a catastrophe."

"Wait a minute," said Teresa. "I've got to see this."

Vortrum looked out the window as he waited with the phone at his ear. He tried to spot the spaceship that was spreading all this poison, but he decided it must be too high up to be seen.

Teresa came back on the phone. "Vortrum, that's not poison, it's snow! Go back to sleep. After breakfast, I'll take you sledding on the golf course. Your space suit's waterproof, isn't it? Wear that. See you later."

Vortrum stared out the window for a while after she'd hung up. It wasn't poison? Snow. He'd never heard of snow on his planet.

I handed the notebook back to Gus. "It's funny," I said. Sometimes it depressed me that Gus was such a better writer than I was. He had good ideas, and when he wrote about Vortrum and Teresa, they sounded alive. When I wrote about them, they seemed like paper dolls that I was moving around the page. Gus never complained, but next to his, my chapters were dull.

"We should go for a walk," Gus said.

"Us? Now?"

"While it's still snowing."

Gus was already pulling on a sweater, so I went down to get my boots and coat.

We walked for an hour, going nowhere special. The store windows had their Christmas decorations up. My favorite was the moving Santa in the florist's window. He waved, turned, and gave a little bow. Then he did it all over again. Every year he got a little dustier, and his suit had faded to pink, but I loved him.

"When will they put the trees on the streetlights?" Gus asked.

"December first. Let's sit on the curb and watch them come on. We'll bring Sebastian."

"I decided what to make Sebastian for Christmas," Gus said. "It's a combination zoo and stable made from a packing crate. I'm putting cages in one half and stalls in the other. Then I'm cutting up an old towel for horse blankets and rubbing cloths. I found plastic animals and little buckets at the hobby shop, and I'm putting rice and Grape-nuts in plastic boxes for the animals' food."

I was trying to catch snowflakes on my tongue. I hardly felt the tinge of cold, they melted so fast. "Catherine would like that. She loves horses," I said.

When we turned around to go home, the snow started to stick. Gus tried to scrape enough off the back of a car to make a snowball, but it was too powdery to pack.

The weeks between Thanksgiving and Christmas were my favorite time at Miss Ayers. The school was decorated with fir branches and holly, pots of poinsettias in the windows, wreaths the size of truck tires on the front doors, and we got out of class early most afternoons to practice for the Christmas program.

After rehearsal Wednesday, I took the late bus home. It was dark when the bus driver let me off at the corner. A few houses were trimmed with Christmas lights. I wished we decorated our house with outdoor lights. On Christmas Eve, Mom put the tree in the front window and left the curtains open, but that's as far as she'd go. I wanted to outline the windows and the front door with colored lights. I even liked the plastic light-up Santa and Frosty statues in the front yard of the corner house.

At our house, the Llewellyns' lights were on upstairs, but the rest of the house was dark. We needed to reset the timer for the front-door lights so they'd come on sooner now that it got dark so early.

I missed Emma most after school. I hated being the first one home to a dark house. Even if you rush in and turn on the lights, the rooms feel empty until someone else gets there. You notice your reflection in the windows and imagine that people outside see everything you're doing. Before, when Emma was there, I could look up the street on my way home, and see the lights on in our apartment. I knew I'd come in and she'd call "Hello!"

I couldn't imagine living alone, always being the first one home. No wonder people have dogs and cats. Big furry dogs to hug. Or talking birds—a parrot. You could teach your dog to push the light switches and train your parrot to say, "Hello, sweetheart. Have a nice day?" But you'd still have to start dinner yourself.

I stopped at the top of the steps and fished for my keys in the pocket of my bookbag. They were buried in the pencils and run-out pens I kept forgetting to throw out. The front-door lock was sticky, and you had to get the key in just right. It finally turned and I pushed open the door.

That's when he grabbed me. He twisted my arm and pushed me inside, kicking the door shut behind us. He shoved me ahead of him into the hall. I started to scream but he jammed his fist in my mouth and twisted my arm harder. He knocked me onto the floor in the corner behind the stairs and tied a cloth over my mouth. I couldn't see him, he stayed behind me, but I heard him panting.

He pulled my arms over my head and tied them at the wrists. Then he pulled up my coat and buried my head with it. The floor was cold and dusty. I sneezed and he punched my back, hard. I wondered why he didn't take my bag and run. I only had four dollars and some change in my wallet. Maybe he wanted the keys to the apartment.

I realized I was holding my breath. He was still panting. But he hadn't been running. If he'd run, I would have heard his footsteps on the sidewalk. He must have been walking very softly, following me, and crept up behind me when I was looking for the keys.

Then I heard the key in the front-door lock. He heard it, too, and kicked my legs out of his way in a rush for the door. He knocked against the door as it opened, and it crashed into the wall.

"What the hell!" Matt Llewellyn yelled. I heard footsteps pounding down the steps. "Gus, grab him."

I tried to cry out but the cloth muffled the sound so I kicked the floor with my feet. Matt heard and came around behind the stairs. "Miranda, my God!" He helped me up and untied my mouth and my hands. "What happened? Are you all right?" he asked.

I kept sobbing, relieved, ashamed, shaking. I started to hiccup. Gus came back in and yelled up the stairs. "Mom, help! Miranda's hurt!"

I leaned against the wall. My stomach flopped over again and again, heaving up air.

Carol rushed downstairs. "What happened?" she asked.

"Some guy attacked Miranda," Matt said. "He had her tied up behind the stairs. When we came home, he ran out."

Carol took my hand and led me upstairs, hugging me and stroking my face.

"It's okay, sweetheart. It's all over. It's okay."

When we got upstairs to the Llewellyns', Carol took me into the kitchen and sat me in the rocker by the window. Matt led Gus and Sebastian out and closed the door.

"Honey, what did he do to you?" She held both my hands and looked at me closely.

"He snuck up behind me as I was opening the door. He

119

covered my mouth. I couldn't yell. Then Matt and Gus came home and he ran out. I never saw him."

"Is that all that happened? Nothing more?"

I knew what she meant. I shook my head.

"We have to call the police," she said.

"*No!*" I said. I didn't want to talk to strangers.

"Honey, we have to. It's important. We have to file a report."

She tucked a blanket around me. Gus came in and sat beside me. Sebastian, looking worried, brought me his bear to hold. I could hear Carol calling my mother and then the police. I hoped Mom would come home first.

She must have taken a cab. I was sipping tea when I heard her running up the stairs. She hurried into the kitchen, banging her briefcase against the counter. She hugged me hard, pressing my face against the scratchy tweed of her coat. Having her so near, smelling her perfume, and feeling her hands stroking my hair made me cry again. She knelt in front of me and held my face in her hands. She was crying, too.

"Oh, baby, what a stinking, lousy thing to have happen. Don't be frightened, sweetheart, we're all here, and we'll stay with you. Carol, you called the police?"

"Matt or Gus might be able to identify the man," Carol said.

"Did you get a good look at him?" Mom asked them.

"No. It happened too fast," Matt said.

"He was shorter than me, but I didn't see his face," Gus said.

120

"The bastard," my mother said. She stayed next to me, holding my hand, until the police rang the front doorbell. Carol went down. We could hear her pointing out the space behind the stairs as they came in. I couldn't tell from the footsteps how many had come. It was only one man and a woman. The woman smiled at me.

I told them what I'd told Carol. It was embarrassing telling it again, this time with Mom, Matt, and Gus there, too, and the police. Sebastian was in the living room watching cartoons. I was talking very quickly.

"A medical exam won't be necessary," the policewoman said.

Mom nodded.

"We'd like you and the kids to come down to the station and look through the books," the policeman said to Matt. "You might be able to identify him."

Mom led me down to our apartment and ran a hot tub. "Lie there and soak, sweetheart. Try to let yourself relax." I lay in the tub but I didn't relax. My back ached from where he punched me, and my arm from being twisted. When I closed my eyes I remembered the cold floor, and the fear.

When I came out, Mom had made soup, and she'd unpacked my favorite Christmas decoration and set it in the middle of the dining room table. It was carved out of wood, with windmill blades on the top. In the center was a nativity scene, Mary, Joseph, and the baby in the manger, with the ox and the donkey. Then, in tiers, other figures moved around them—the shepherds and sheep in one circle, the

Wise Men and camels in another, angels playing music in a third, and finally, Santa, the reindeer, and some children. When we lit the candles, the circles rotated. I watched it turn as I stirred my soup.

Later, Mom, Gus, and Matt came with me to the police station. I don't know why I had to go since I never saw his face. We sat in front of a book of photos while the policeman turned the pages.

"He was younger than these guys," Gus said.

They took out another book and began flipping pages again. These faces were younger but just as scary. Gus kept shaking his head. Finally they let us go home.

I was glad he didn't find the face. Whoever it was, I didn't want to see him. It was scary enough to remember being tied, and punched. It would be much worse to have his face in my mind.

We got home after ten. When I went to bed, Mom stayed in my room and rubbed my back gently, moving her palm in big circles. She left the lamp on my dresser on, and I could see her shadow on the wall.

"Tomorrow, you'll be worn out. Sleep in and we'll go to the museum for lunch."

"What will you do about work?"

"I told them I'd be out. No problem." She kept on rubbing my back.

I closed my eyes. She traced gentle circles on my back. Then, very softly, she sang a lullaby she used to sing when I was small enough to sit in her lap and rock, about a shepherd counting his sheep to make sure every single one was safe.

13

When I woke up Thursday morning, I could hear Mom
talking to her office on the phone. She hung up as soon as
I came into the living room. "Good morning," she said,
patting the couch beside her. I sat down cross-legged on
the cushion. The sun was out and the house was quiet.
Mom pointed to a vase of roses on the coffee table and
handed me the card.

*For Miranda, with all our love, Carol, Matt, Gus, and
Sebastian.* No one had ever sent me flowers before. I picked
the smallest rose out of the vase and stroked the petals. It
smelled sweeter than Emma's rose powder.

"I called school," Mom said. "I want them to under-stand. It's nothing you should feel ashamed about."

I didn't answer. I watched the sun bounce off the photos on the mantel. Why should anyone have to know? I wasn't ashamed, I just didn't want everybody talking about me.

We went to the Museum of Fine Arts after breakfast. The galleries were practically empty. I always liked the Impressionists, but they didn't interest me this time. I was sleepwalking through the big rooms, gazing at the pictures.

Mom read the map carefully. "Miranda, look," she pointed to a shaded space. "The new Japanese garden is finished. Let's see if it's open in the winter." We found the door to the garden next to a room of giant Buddhas. The guard nodded when Mom asked if we could go out.

The sun was pale, but the walls kept out the wind. At first we stood on the steps looking out at the white stones, the old bell, the trees, and the frozen pond. The stones were raked in a pattern of waving lines, symmetrical as ripples. The trunks and branches of the trees were bent like very old men and women frozen in a dance.

I sat on a bench in the corner and stared out at the pattern of the stones and the orange bittersweet berries next to the bell. The wall guarded me, and the emptiness of the garden calmed me. If there had been a tiny house, I could have lived there forever.

While I stayed in the garden, Mom went to pick out Christmas cards in the gift shop. Then we had lunch up-stairs. Our table overlooked the garden, so I had more time to look at it.

All day, I kept close to Mom. When we got home, she

cast on forty stitches of knitting for me and I started a scarf, gray-blue wool, just knit, no purl, so I didn't have to concentrate. Mom stacked kindling and logs in the fireplace and lit a fire. I sat on the couch and watched the flames change color as the wood burned down.

Gus came by after school. "Want to go skating? The pond in the park is frozen."

"No, thanks," I said.

"Maybe tomorrow," Gus said.

I nodded.

When I heard him go out with Sebastian, I wished I'd said yes. I loved to skate with Gus. I copied the way he lifted his feet and stepped through his turns. But soon it would be dark. I didn't want to be out after dark.

The next day, Friday, I went back to school.

"Nobody knows what happened except Miss Campion and Miss Rathbone," Mom said. "They've both promised to keep it private."

"Were you sick?" Catherine asked. I nodded. "Why didn't you call me? We had a lab in Hygiene and I had to work with Cynthia One." Catherine sliced her hand across her throat.

"What was the lab?"

"We have fertilized eggs, three for each team. Yesterday, we took a piece of the shell off. The embryo was just beginning to form. Next week we'll do another, and see how much it's developed. Join my team so we'll outnumber Cynthia," Catherine said. "All she did was complain about her nails."

We walked upstairs to Rathbone's class. I thought of

telling Catherine about the museum, the garden, and the Buddhas. But if I told her about the museum, she'd think it was strange that my mother let me stay home.

Miss Rathbone handed out our writing folders. I looked over the piece I'd been working on, about our summer cottage. I couldn't get going again. Miss Rathbone noticed. She crooked her index finger at me. I snaked between the desks up to the front and sat in the chair beside her desk. I hadn't had a writing conference with her in weeks.

"Try something new," she suggested.

"Like what?"

"You're the only one who can answer that." Miss Rathbone smiled. She'd been saying that since September. But my mind was as empty as the blackboard. "Just let yourself drift. Put down whatever comes to mind. Use the time to explore."

I nodded but I knew I wouldn't. If I let my mind wander, it might go back to Wednesday night.

I decided to write about my grandmother's hair. She tinted it ice blue, and had it piled and sprayed into a helmet every week.

All day, I pretended that nothing had happened. I smiled, and tried to listen, and acted as normal as I could. Every so often, I'd remember something—the way he knocked me down or tied my hands—and I'd shiver. I got half the problems wrong in math, stupid mistakes.

In every class, I looked out the window. Bare trees, bare ground, gray sky. I wished it would snow so hard we could all go home. Snow would cover up everything.

Friday night I woke up screaming, with Mom sitting beside me trying to calm me.

"It's okay, sweetheart. You're all right. I'm here. Nothing can hurt you." She held me in her arms. "It was just a dream. A bad dream. It's all over now. Do you think you can get back to sleep?" she asked.

"No," I said.

"Come into my room. I think you'll get sleepy soon."

She tucked me in to the other side of her big bed. Then she got in bed and turned off the light on her side. "Try to sleep, baby. I'm right here if you need me."

Her voice was groggy. I didn't want to keep her up. I lay on my back looking up at the ceiling. Why did this have to happen to me? Why did he pick my house? I hated being a girl. I hated breasts. I hated the prospect of getting my period. If I'd been a boy, this wouldn't have happened. Nobody ever bothered Gus. Boys don't watch how they sit. Nobody stares at their chests. They don't have to be afraid.

Upstairs, in his attic room, Gus was probably dreaming a safe, ordinary dream, about space, maybe, or soccer. Sebastian was probably dreaming about Christmas. That's all he could talk about. They didn't have to worry. For boys, growing up meant getting stronger. It meant riding your bike anywhere you wanted, staying out after dark if you felt like it. For girls, growing up meant being careful, being afraid. I wished I was Sebastian's age again. I wished I was a boy.

When Gus and I were little, we used to go to a wading

127

pool in the park with a statue of a fat baby boy sitting on a dolphin. Water sprayed out of the dolphin's head. We'd splash and paddle in the shallow water, wearing underpants or swimsuits. I liked to wear boys' swim trunks just like Gus's because they had pockets. When I found a penny or a bottle cap I'd put it in my pocket. One day an old woman in a baggy flowered dress stood by the side of the fountain watching us. After a while she went up to Mom and Carol. "Put a top on that child and cover her breasts," she yelled, pointing a skinny wrinkled finger at me. I looked at myself and I looked at Gus. I couldn't see any difference between my chest and his. But after that, Mom made me wear a girl's tank suit, and I finally gave up complaining about it.

Thinking of Sebastian, I tiptoed back into my room and found my old stuffed dog, Mr. Bones. I carried him back to Mom's room and inched into bed, trying not to wake her. She snored, a cross between a sigh and a whistle. Her back was warm and solid beside me. I pulled the covers up to my chin and hugged soft, familiar, lumpy Mr. Bones. I ran my fingers back and forth along the silky edge of the blanket trim and hoped I wouldn't dream again.

14

Saturday afternoon Gus came downstairs while I was fooling around on the piano, picking out the notes for the snow dance in *The Nutcracker*. He stood leaning by the door while I finished. Gus never minded waiting.

"Want to go skating?" he asked. "Sebastian's going to his friend Wolf's birthday party."

"Sebastian has a friend named Wolf?"

"From preschool. It's short for Wolfgang. Sebastian wants to change his name to Fox. Mom said no, of course."

Gus waited for me while I changed into my long underwear. When we reached the park, I was glad I'd added the extra layer. The wind blew over the empty flowerbeds and lawns so hard we bent our heads. At the pond, pine trees blocked the wind, but only a handful of skaters criss-crossed the ice.

We laced up our skates and stowed our boots under the bench. Gus stepped out on the ice without hesitation. I inched over to the edge, then stepped out, taking baby steps. One foot slipped out fast and I was on my behind before I left the shore. I dusted off the dry frost and wobbled toward the middle of the pond. At a rink, I could grab the rail and hope nobody noticed how bad a skater I was, but at the pond I teetered around wishing I was invisible. After a while I let myself slide a little every few steps.

Gus skated with long strides, his hands in his jacket pockets, rocking from side to side. He slowed down and skated alongside of me for a while.

"You're stiff, that's the trouble," he said after one circle of the pond. "You're afraid to fall. Bend your knees and put your hands down in front of you as if you were pressing on a table. Good. Now keep them there. They throw you off balance when you wave them around."

I tried to follow his instructions. Step, together, glide. Step, together, glide. Press down. My feet felt more solid.

"That's it," Gus said. "You've got it. Try that for a while and then I'll show you some more."

"When did you learn this?" I asked.

"Last year I came down here on Saturday mornings when you had ballet. An old guy showed me what to do. If I see him again, I'll introduce you."

130

Gradually more skaters came out on the pond. Four hot-shot high school boys played tag with each other, dodging in among the slower skaters. One wore speed skates with extra long blades. I tried to keep over to the edge, out of their way. They grabbed one girl's hat and swung it by its pom-pom like a lasso. They pulled another girl's scarf, dragging her halfway around the pond, stopping only when the guard warned them. I was glad I was wearing a hood.

Gus came up alongside me. "Want some hot chocolate?" he asked.

We bought hot chocolate and a bag of roasted chestnuts, then sat on a log. The cocoa was so hot I had to sip it slowly. I watched the other skaters circle the pond, some smooth as dancers, others stiff-legged, flailing for balance. Even though it was only a little after four, the sky was turning navy blue and the lights of the taller buildings glowed above the dark tree shapes. Gus peeled me a chestnut.

"We should go home soon," I said. The darkness made me nervous.

"A few more times around, then we'll go, okay?"

We stepped back onto the ice and Gus skated off with a wave. I wobbled until I got my balance and my courage back. I concentrated on my steps and glides. Just as I was making the turn, the boy with speed skates cut the corner fast and knocked me on my stomach. The fall pushed my breath out and I scraped my cheek. For a few seconds, I lay sprawled on the ice trying to get my breath. Then I heard Gus's voice. "Miranda, are you okay?"

I started to cry. I was facedown in almost the same position as that other night, and Gus was there again. I felt so awkward and ashamed. I brushed away Gus's hand, and got to my feet by myself. "I told you we should go home," I said. I don't know why I was angry at him. He hadn't done anything. But I couldn't help it.

We walked home in the dark, neither of us speaking. I kept my hands in my pockets and my arms close to my sides, careful not to even brush against Gus's arm. At the house, he stood in the hall while I opened the door to my apartment.

"I'm sorry," he said. "I should've stayed with you."

"It's not your fault, I should've seen him coming."

Gus kicked the toe of his boot against the stair. "You know what I hate? The way those guys always travel in a gang. They think they can do anything. They make me feel like a jerk."

"Why?"

"I guess they scare me. I hate that. I wish I had the guts to stand up to them."

"You did on Halloween."

"Not soon enough, and I didn't do anything today." He leaned against the wall cracking his knuckles. I didn't know what to say. My cheek hurt and I wanted to take off my heavy clothes. I was worn out from my own feelings. I didn't have room for his.

"Want to play cards after dinner? Or watch TV?" Gus said.

I said no. I knew he was disappointed, but I didn't feel

like being with him. It wasn't his fault, but he reminded me of everything that had happened.

That night, back in my own bed, I had another nightmare. I was running down a long narrow hall. I was afraid to turn around. The hall opened out into a field and I was running in mud. I didn't know where I was and I was sure I'd slip.

Mom shook me awake. "You were screaming again, honey. It's okay. It was just a dream." She wiped my face with the edge of the sheet. "I think you should sleep in my room until these dreams stop," she said.

The last time I'd slept with my mother for more than one night at a time, I was four and afraid of robbers. I thought they'd climb up the fire escape outside my window. Every time the breeze blew the curtains, I was sure a robber was coming to steal me. I slept in Mom's bed until she bought special window locks and moved me back into my own room. "Robbers don't take little girls," she said. "They take silver dishes and we don't have any so you don't have to worry." I believed her.

Monday, we had a rehearsal for *The Little Match Girl*, the middle school holiday play. Girls with speaking parts had been rehearsing since early in November. Danielle, the sixth grader who sat next to me in study hall, was the Match Girl, and tall Louise was her grandmother. Millie, Catherine, and I had nonspeaking parts as children in a family. The Match Girl sees us through the wall of our house when she strikes her matches. I couldn't figure out how they would show her looking right through a wall.

"They do it with lights and a curtain," Catherine explained. "At first the curtain looks like a wall, but it's really transparent. When they turn on the lights behind it, the audience can see our scene."

Catherine, Millie, and I had to do every movement slowly, in an exaggerated way, so the audience would know what we were doing—decorating the tree, playing games, eating dinner. Catherine was chosen to put the star on top of the tree. She climbed a stepladder and pretended to lose her balance just as she put the star on top.

"Don't flail!" said Miss Avondell, the drama teacher.

"I'm trying not to fall," said Catherine.

"You look like a windmill. Try to totter more."

"More totter, less flail," Catherine repeated.

Miss Avondell didn't laugh. "Try it again, Catherine."

Catherine stuck her tongue out at me and climbed the ladder again. This time, she tried not to wave her arms, but she was so off balance that if she hadn't grabbed the ladder she would have fallen. She tried it again and managed to sway at the top, tottering only a little.

After we practiced singing the carols a few times, we watched Danielle rehearse her Match Girl lines. She was a good choice for the part, with bony wrists and knees that jutted out and her skin so pale the veins showed on the sides of her forehead. It was easy to imagine her standing in a snowy street a hundred years ago. When she approached people to sell her matches, she hesitated, ashamed and afraid.

She crouched down as if trying to get out of the wind, and spoke to herself, "I can't go home. I haven't sold a single match. Father will beat me, I'm sure. It's as cold as this at home, besides."

In our first scene, we played games by a stove. When Danielle lit her second match, our scene had changed to a dinner table covered with a white tablecloth. Again, Catherine had the funny part. She spilled her cup reaching across the table, and was scolded. She stamped her foot, then swished to the end of the room and stood in a corner, peeking around and making rude faces.

After the third match had burned, the light went out behind the curtain and our scene disappeared. A small spotlight, meant to be a shooting star, moved across the top of the stage. "Someone is dying," the Match Girl said. "Grandma always said a shooting star is a soul traveling up to heaven."

She pulled her shawl around her, looked at the matches left in her pocket, then slowly lit one more match. A figure entered through the back curtain, smiled, and held out her arms. "Grandmother! Take me with you!" the Match Girl said, frantically lighting match after match to see her grandmother's face.

Standing backstage, I cried for her. Catherine shoved a Kleenex in my hand.

On the bus after rehearsal, Catherine said, "Danielle's good, isn't she?"

I nodded. I didn't want to talk about it much. I wished we could pull the Match Girl through the curtain into our half of the stage where she wouldn't be alone. "It's sad," I said.

"It doesn't even have a happy ending," Catherine said.

135

"I think it does. She's not alone anymore. She's with her grandmother."

"They're dead," Catherine said. "That's not very happy."

"It's better than being cold and lonely," I said.

The bus left me off at the corner. The sidewalk was empty. I sang "Hark, the Herald Angels" to myself, but halfway down the block, I thought I heard footsteps behind me. I didn't want to turn around. I ran the rest of the way and panted up the steps of my house. My keys were somewhere in the bottom of my bag again. I couldn't find them quickly enough. So I pushed the Llewellyns' doorbell and kept my finger on the button. When they buzzed me in, I opened the door, crying a little.

"Miranda?" Carol called down. "Are you okay?"

"I couldn't find my keys," I said.

"Come up and have some tea."

I didn't want her to see me crying. "I'll come up when I've changed."

I unlocked the door to our apartment and went through the rooms flipping on lights. But even when I pulled down the living room shades and turned on the TV, I couldn't shake the fear.

The Brady Bunch were yakking. The housekeeper made me lonely for Emma, and thinking of Emma made me cry again. I couldn't go up to the Llewellyns' with red eyes, so I stayed on the couch watching TV and sniffling until Mom came home.

"What's wrong, baby? Did something happen at school?"

I shook my head. For a moment I thought of blaming my tears on a sad TV show but I couldn't make up a story that fast. "I got scared coming home. The house was dark. It's stupid."

Mom shut off the TV and sat down beside me.

"Honey, it's not stupid at all. It's natural. I should have thought more about this. It was stupid of *me*."

"I wish Emma could come back," I said.

"We can't pull her back now that she's settled."

"If you told her what happened, she'd come back," I said, angry at myself for being a baby. "You don't care about me. You're glad she's gone. I hate being afraid. I hate having no one here and the rooms all dark."

Mom slumped down and leaned her head against the back of the couch. "I'm not glad she's gone, really I'm not. Life would be a lot easier if she'd stayed. I don't want you to be afraid. We both know she'd come back in a minute if we told her. But I don't think it's fair to put her in that position. I don't think it would work, having her back. Sometimes you can't turn things back, you can't unsay things. That's how it is with me and Emma."

I was still mad at Mom. She could apologize. If she loved me, she'd do it. She'd call Emma and beg her to come back. If Emma came back, the house wouldn't be dark after school. She'd even meet me at the corner and walk me down the block. She'd insist on it. That made me remember the other side of Emma—the Emma who still treated me like a four-year-old. Pull up your socks. Change your underwear. Finish your milk. Brush your teeth. Get your hair off your face.

"We'll think of something," Mom said. "I thought going upstairs to the Llewellyns' would work. But we'll think of something. You're too big for a baby-sitter, right?" She patted my knee. I nodded.

Mom got up. "I'm going to start dinner. I'll keep thinking."

Halfway through her bowl of chili, she said, "Tina! Let's invite Tina to live with us. It'll get her out of that dump. I think she just works mornings at the nursing home so she could be here in the afternoons."

"We can ask her," I said.

15

Mom called Tina. She'd just had a fight with the High Spirits Jazz Quartet over a pot of spaghetti sauce left on the stove so long it sprouted a garden of mold. "I'll be packed by tomorrow," she said.

We drove over to get her as soon as Mom got home from work. Tina insisted on giving us a tour. "You have to see it. The Board of Health might condemn it any day and then you'd never know what you missed."

We followed her upstairs to the second-floor apartment. The living room, shaped like a shoebox with a window at the far end, was furnished with a mattress covered with an Indian spread, a black beanbag chair with an X of silver tape covering a rip, and two faded green director's chairs. Stereo speakers stood in two corners and between them, on the floor, a cassette player sat on top of a crate of tapes. A keyboard on skinny metal legs blocked the window.

A dozen empty soda cans were scattered on the floor, the windowsill, the arms of the director's chairs. An undershirt, a black leather jacket, and a saxophone case were piled on one director's chair. The other held phone books and a jar of peanut butter. We walked past the kitchen on our way to Tina's room. A young man, wearing only a pair of jeans, sat on the counter eating pizza from a box.

"That's Max, the drummer. We're not speaking. Nobody else is home."

Tina's room was a cell with a window facing an air shaft. She'd painted it yellow, and she'd stapled up three van Gogh prints, sunflowers and irises. But even with all that color, the room was sad. "I'm glad you're coming to our house," Mom said.

I hoped that didn't hurt Tina's feelings. "I like your prints," I said.

"Want them? No reason to leave them for the slobs." She pulled the prints off the wall and rolled them up with a rubber band.

We carried Tina's bags downstairs. Max didn't offer to help. He didn't say good-bye either.

When we showed Tina Emma's old bedroom, she stood in the middle of the rug and turned around, looking at the curtains, the oak bureau, the armchair, the curved mirror.

"It's all yours," Mom said. "Use the living room, the TV, the piano, whatever you like. You'll have to tell us what you like to eat."

"Yogurt, mostly, but I'll do the shopping. That's part of the deal, right? I take care of the shopping and cooking. I finish work at noon and my classes are all at night so I'll have time."

The next day, Tina was home when I got home from school. I saw the lights in the living room windows as I walked up the block, and when I opened the front door, I heard rock and roll.

"I used to like jazz, but after four months in that apartment, I need a break," Tina said. "Want to do some stretches? Pull on a leotard or a pair of shorts."

She had on a pair of black tights and a T-shirt, so I changed into tights, too. We started with running in place, then side bends and bouncing straight from the hips. Tina made up a dance that was a cross between jumping jacks and a cancan. We tried to do it for the whole song. I was glad to lie down on the carpet for the next set of exercises.

"Do you do this every day?" I asked.

"If I don't take a dance class, I do. I took ballet when I was little, but I wasn't the right shape so I switched to modern in high school. Dancing's good for acting."

"I used to take ballet, but I quit. Maybe I'll start again. But not ballet, some other kind of dance."

"Come to class with me and see what you like. Jazz is faster, modern's more creative. For me, that is. And there's tap, too. I never learned tap, but I'd like to try sometime."

She looked at her watch. "I've got to start dinner. You probably have homework, don't you?"

I did my homework in my room. Tina's music filtered in through the door. Emma never played rock and roll. Emma in a leotard! That made me smile. Then I felt disloyal. Emma was different, that's all.

"Dinner's ready," Tina called. She'd set the dining room table, and lit candles. A salad bowl, a basket of pita bread, and a covered casserole dish sat on the table.

"This looks elegant," Mom said. She'd come home while I was doing my homework.

Tina rubbed her palms together, then motioned for us to sit down. "I found this recipe in my natural food cookbook. I've never tried it before," she said.

She took the cover off the casserole and we all looked in. Four long fat shapes filled the dish. They were browned on top, and the underneath looked greenish.

"What is it?" Animal, vegetable, or mineral? I wanted to ask.

"Zucchini Canoes. They're stuffed with rice and cheese." Tina spooned one onto each plate. "There's an extra for anyone who wants it," she said.

I was sure it wouldn't be me.

Mom and Tina actually ate their canoes. I cut mine up and squished it around, hoping it would look as if I'd swallowed some. I did eat one small forkful. The taste was bland, but the texture was squishy with bumps of rice. I washed it down with a gulp of water.

"So tell me what happened, Miranda," Tina said. "If

you don't mind talking about it." She tilted her head to one side as I described the attack, and nodded with each detail. Her college roommate had been held up in an elevator, she told me. "He took her watch and her wallet but he finally let her go. Have you ever been mugged, Aunt Fran?"

"Not mugged, but I've been harassed. Men have said the usual obscene things a few times."

"Like what?" Tina and I asked at the same time, and laughed at our curiosity.

Mom grinned, embarrassed. "Come on, you two, you know."

"*I* don't," I said.

"They say stupid things like 'Hey, baby, busy tonight?' Sometimes it's more specific."

"Like what?" I begged her to tell me more, but she wouldn't.

"It happens to everybody," Tina said. "One time in the grocery store when I was about fifteen, I held the door open for this old guy with a cane. A cane! I mean, he must have been eighty-five, and he said, 'Thank you,' and then he offered me five dollars to come home with him and strip. I wished I'd let the door drop in his face."

"Last year Catherine was on the ferry and a man waved his penis at her," I said.

"Did she wave back?" Tina said.

Mom choked on the water she was sipping. "That's awful! What did she do?"

"She told the captain and he made the guy leave her

alone. And later, she told her mother. Her mother said it happens a lot to girls our age."

Mom and Tina nodded.

"It happened to my friend when she was on crutches with her leg in a cast. She said, 'Gimme a break and put that away,' " Tina said.

"It happened to me when I was eight months pregnant and shaped like a dirigible," Mom said.

"Pregnant with me?" I asked.

She nodded. "Who else?"

"Why do men do it?" I asked.

Mom and Tina shook their heads. "I haven't a clue," Mom said. "It's usually harmless."

"But it's still creepy," Tina said. "Like obscene phone calls and porno magazines. It's all sleazy and it makes me mad! As if women aren't even people."

"It makes all of us mad," Mom said. "There's not much we can do except ignore them and keep going."

After Tina moved in, I didn't mind the afternoons. I still slept in Mom's room at night, but I didn't dream for several nights.

"What's your cousin like?" Catherine asked, when we were sitting on the stage waiting for rehearsal to start. "Is she pretty?"

"I guess so. She's got brown hair. She usually pulls it up on top of her head in a knot, and it falls out a little. She wears a lot of eye makeup, dark pencil and gray shiny stuff she smudges on."

"Is she weird, like Miss Leopold?"

144

I thought of Miss Leopold's chiffon scarves and dance skirts. "No. Miss Leopold looks like something that's been up in the attic for a long time. Tina looks brand-new."

Gus was also interested in Tina. "She's so different from Emma," he said one afternoon when we were playing double solitaire in the living room.

I hadn't seen much of Gus since the attack. I wasn't mad at him. But I felt different around him than I used to. It wasn't his fault. But I felt uncomfortable with him. I stayed away from Matt Llewellyn, too. For once, I was glad I went to a girls' school, and I was glad Mom hadn't married again. It was easier to stay clear of men, that's all. Even Gus. I noticed how deep his voice was and the size of his hands. His feet were enormous. His sneakers were half again the size of mine. Maybe if he'd been smaller, I wouldn't have felt uncomfortable. He reminded me of the attack, and how easy it had been for that man to hold me down and twist my arms. Gus would never do anything like that, but he could if he wanted to.

Friday afternoon, Gus asked if I wanted to sleep over. "Theater of Thrills has a Christmas special," he said. "*Vampire Elves and the Reindeers' Revenge*. We can make popcorn. Maybe we can work on *Alien Attraction* after dinner."

I thought about it. I hadn't been up to Gus's room in two weeks. The window seat and the notebooks seemed like dusty memories.

Gus sat on the piano stool with his shoulders hunched forward and his hands tucked under his thighs. He watched me as if he already knew what I'd say but he didn't understand why. Neither did I. How could I do this to my oldest friend?

"No, thanks," I said. "Catherine's sleeping over." I hadn't asked her yet, and I hoped she'd say yes. Even if she didn't, I could say her mother changed her mind. I'd never lied to Gus before. But I didn't want to sleep over. I couldn't explain why. "Next week's the Christmas program at school. Maybe you could come," I said. It was a peace offering, something to make up for the lie.

He nodded.

"Tina might come, too. She's helping me with my part. She's going to help Catherine tonight." The lie was growing. "Catherine's got a bigger part."

"Why don't you both come up and watch Theater of Thrills?"

Just then the phone rang. Answering it gave me a minute to think. Catherine would love a chance to be with Gus. She still asked about him. But if she couldn't sleep over, then I'd have to go up by myself.

The call was for Tina. I went back to the living room. "I'll ask Catherine. She doesn't usually like horror shows."

Gus smiled. The corners of his eyes made fans of wrinkles. I remembered how much I liked him.

Catherine couldn't sleep over, but Tina asked me to go to a movie with her, so I told Gus I couldn't come upstairs. I felt guilty, so I invited him to the movie, too. But he had to stay with Sebastian. Maybe it was my imagination, but he sounded glad to turn me down.

16

Saturday morning I met Catherine downtown. The sign on top of Ferne's Department Store said, EIGHT SHOPPING DAYS LEFT. I'd already bought Catherine's present, a tiny stuffed pony with a red bridle and saddle.

"Let's go to the basement," Catherine said. She liked making decisions.

"Too crowded," I said.

"Every store's going to be crowded today," Catherine said. "Look at all these people. It's only ten o'clock! Crowded and crowded, what's the difference?"

"The basement's the worst. People grab stuff from right

in front of you. They'd break your arm for a blouse."

"So push back. Step on their feet! Then say, 'Oh, I'm sorry.' Let's at least start with the basement. If it's too packed, we'll go upstairs and have some cocoa and a raisin bun at Frenchy's."

I followed Catherine across Tremont Street. She plodded through the crowd like a snowplow. I stayed close behind, in her wake.

I still needed gifts for Mom, Tina, Sebastian, and, of course, Gus. There wouldn't be anything in the basement for Gus. He didn't like clothes. I usually knew weeks ahead of time what to get him, but this time I couldn't decide.

We pushed through the double doors and paused at the top of the stairs. The basement stretched out below us, one huge room with tables of sweaters, scarves, shirts, pants, underwear, ties, jewelry, shoes, baby clothes, even towels and sheets. A sign above each table told the contents. Name Brand Sweaters. Misses' Lingerie.

"Let's try the scarves. Then the lingerie," Catherine said.

At the scarf table, a salesgirl was trying to keep things folded, while all around the table women picked up scarves and shook them out to see the patterns. The salesgirl would snatch up the scarves when the ladies dropped them, and fold them all over again. She didn't say anything, just glared and cracked her gum.

Catherine picked up a red and purple scarf and flipped it open. In the middle was an ugly golden lion. I tried to ignore the salesgirl. I held up a scarf with green and blue stripes, then another with purple irises. Mom loved irises.

She wore scarves a lot with her business clothes. This one was a little more expensive than I'd planned on, but it was big and very soft.

"It's silk," Catherine said.

I decided to buy it.

We moved on to the jewelry counter. Catherine found a tie clasp with crossed tennis rackets on it for her father. I found a tropical fish pin for Tina. In the children's section, I found Sebastian a pair of mittens. Rudolph's nose turned red when you wore them in cold weather. Catherine wanted a pair, too, but the sizes were all too small.

"I've got to find something for my mother," she said. "Let's try lingerie."

I'd never looked at lingerie before. Mom always bought me cotton underpants, three to a package, all white or pink-blue-yellow. We'd gone to the lingerie department last spring to buy me a bra, but I didn't look at anything else. I pretended I wasn't there while Mom and the saleslady discussed sizes and types.

Catherine started at the camisole table. She pulled out a red top with a black lace V in front and held it up against her parka. "What do you think?"

I couldn't believe she'd put it up against her front like that. The next one she tried was black, with a net panel down the middle and on each side. The silky part would just barely have covered her. Who wore these things?

The underpants table was worse. The bikini pants were so tiny I couldn't see any point in wearing them. Some were just two triangles of lace tied together with ribbons.

Catherine showed me a deep rose bikini with beige lace around each leg.

"Do you like it?" she asked.

"For your mother?"

"No, for me! Isn't it pretty?"

"You wouldn't wear that, would you?"

"Sure. Feel it. It's so silky." Catherine measured it against the front of her jeans. I tried not to look around in case someone was watching us.

"You're too young," I said.

"Anyone can wear them. I'm going to buy them."

"You're crazy. What about your mother?"

"It's just underwear. Nobody sees it. I'll be the only one who knows, except you. Come on, let's look at the nightgowns. Maybe I'll find her something there."

She did—a green negligee with black lace trim that belonged in a late-night movie. I couldn't imagine ever buying one for my mother.

The next week we had rehearsal Monday and Tuesday, and dress rehearsal on Wednesday. A senior was in charge of the costumes. "Remember to bring stockings and flats tomorrow. Black patent leather if you've got them. But even ballet slippers will do. Anything's better than these," she said, nodding at Catherine's loafers.

My dress was red, with a wide skirt and a bow at the back. "Can you pull your hair back? It would look more old-fashioned." The costume person handed me a barrette. I tried, but strands slipped out and I had to tuck them behind my ears. I'd get Tina to help on Thursday, I thought.

Dress rehearsal was a mess. Catherine fell off the ladder

when she reached to put the star on the tree. The girl playing the maid dropped the rubber goose. I tripped on my dress and tore out the hem. But Danielle was even better than she'd been before. Maybe it was the set, with the pine trees, the snowflakes falling, and the street dimly lit.

On Thursday, Mom and Tina and all the Llewellyns came to the play. Tina helped me with my hair and my makeup. "You don't want to overdo it," she said, "but you've got to exaggerate a little so we'll see it in the audience." She lined my eyes, put blush on my cheekbones, and lipstick on my lips. She used a curling iron on my hair, and pulled it away from my face, tying it with a black ribbon in back. She loaned me black stockings, too. "These look more old-fashioned. But please, try not to get a run."

The costume girl whistled when I showed up to get dressed. "Who did your makeup?" she asked.

"My cousin. She's an actress."

"She knows what she's doing. I wish I did!" She rolled her eyes around at the mess in the room, then tried to hurry the others. "Come on, you slugs, let's rock and roll."

We took our positions and tried not to whisper. Catherine peeked out the slit in the curtains. Mrs. Drake, the piano player, was playing carols quietly in the background and we could hear people talking and chairs squeaking and scraping as the audience took their seats. "I see Gus," Catherine hissed. Miss Avondell tapped her on the shoulder and motioned her to be quiet and get back in place. I could tell from the way she shook her head that she'd had enough of Catherine this month.

The curtains opened as the chorus hummed "Oh, Come,

Oh, Come, Emmanuel" very slowly. I'd never realized what a sad, waiting song it is. The play went smoothly, the Match Girl trying to sell her matches, the boy stealing the shoe, the scenes with the tree, the stove, and the dinner. When the shooting star spotlight crossed the stage, the audience *aahh*ed, and when the grandmother appeared, someone clapped. Maybe it was Sebastian. I knew he'd hate the Match Girl being so alone. At the end of the play, when Danielle took her bow, people stood up to applaud her, and we clapped, too.

Afterward, we changed out of our costumes and watched the other play from the balcony with the lighting crew. Then everyone was invited to the guest parlor. Catherine hung around with her hands behind her back, ignoring her parents and trying to get a conversation started with Gus. I knew what she was doing, and I figured he did, too. He kept asking me about the snow and the lighting.

Tina wanted to find Danielle and congratulate her, as one actress to another. Matt had Sebastian in his arms, and Carol was patting Sebastian's back. "Honey, it was just a play," she told him. "The little girl isn't really cold. Look, she's over there, drinking cider with her mom and dad."

Sebastian twisted his head to see Danielle. Then, satisfied, he put his head back on his father's shoulder and sucked his thumb.

"We'd better get home," Matt said.

Gus went to get the coats and I went along to help him. Catherine would have come, too, but her mother tapped her on the shoulder. "Catherine, introduce us to Miss Avondell, please," she said. It wasn't a request.

The coatracks were back outside the assembly hall. I led the way past the library, over the bridge above the driveway, into the new wing.

"Is it always this clean?" Gus asked.

"What do you mean?"

"The shiny floors and the walls—there's no writing. Everything's polished. How do they keep it like this?"

"Maids clean it," I told him.

"You're kidding."

"No, really, maids mop and dust and once a week a man named Howard waxes the floors with a big machine. He's the gardener." I could hear how strange it must sound to him.

He whistled. "We have one janitor, Mr. Delaney, who takes care of the whole building. Five hundred kids, four floors, one janitor." Gus ran his hand along the polished-wood rail. "Maids!"

We walked upstairs toward the auditorium.

"You look good in that makeup," Gus said.

"It makes me feel like a clown, sort of."

"It looked great on stage. It's a little much close up, but it still looks nice."

I was pleased. Gus didn't give out compliments often. This might have been the first.

"I think Catherine likes you," I said.

He nodded. "I figured from the way she buzzes around. She's nice, but she's not my type."

I was glad to hear him say it. "I didn't know you had a type."

"Maybe I don't. I don't know what I mean."

"You must have meant something."

"I'm just more comfortable with some people than with others."

"Like who?"

"Come on, Miranda, you're embarrassing me."

He pulled the coats off the hangers and we each carried an armful back to the parlors.

17

I woke up on the morning of the twenty-third worried that I still hadn't found a present for Gus. Mom was hidden under the quilt like a turtle pulled into its shell. She had the day off—a four-day Christmas weekend. The room was much colder than usual. I looked out the window to check the weather and the sill was freezing. The few people on the street hurried by with chins buried in collars, and scarves wrapped around their ears. I dug in my drawer for knee socks and a turtleneck, and found my jeans and thickest sweater in the closet. It was warmer in the kitchen. Tina was drinking coffee in her bathrobe.

"Hi, doll," she said.

"It's cold," I said.

"Sixteen degrees. Blowing down from Canada, and snow's coming. I'm leaving at noon to beat the storm. Want some cocoa? There's more in the saucepan."

I put a muffin in the toaster. "Will Raymond be home for Christmas?"

"Yup. Solo. Helene's in California visiting friends. Ray doesn't sound happy about it. Maybe she's planning to fly the nest. It's my guess that living on a graduate student's budget doesn't suit her taste."

"Wouldn't Ray be sad if she left?" I asked.

Tina shrugged. "Maybe for a while. Maybe not. Didn't she seem clingy to you at Thanksgiving? Always sitting beside him or on his lap. Ugh! Give me some space! Ray's just knocked out by her looks now. He might get tired of the femme fatale routine. I hope they do split up. Then Mom will stop talking about it. Mothers and sons! Believe me, nobody's more possessive than a mother over her baby boy, especially if there's only one. The prince. Nobody's good enough for the prince. Remember the princess and the pea? Believe me, the prince who put her through that was an only son."

It sounded like Tina knew some other only sons.

"Carol's not like that about Gus," I said.

"It comes out when they start to date. Anyway, Gus isn't an only son. She'll be more possessive about Sebastian. He's the baby."

I dribbled honey on my muffin.

Tina frowned at the crossword. "What's a six-letter

156

word for vicious? Where do they get these words? The only things I know are movie titles and names of actors and actresses."

"Tina, what do you think I should get Gus for Christmas?" I asked.

She looked up from the paper. "You haven't gotten him anything yet?"

"I can't think of anything."

"Are you going to eat the other half of that muffin?" She reached over and took it. "Go over to Harvard Square and check all the bookstores. You'll find something. Try the poster departments. There's a good game store, too."

"I'll drive you over." Mom poured a cup of coffee, sat down at the table, and yawned. "I need to shop, too."

"What's a six-letter word for vicious?" Tina asked.

"Lupine," Mom said. "Wolflike."

Tina filled in the letters. "That's amazing, Aunt Fran. How did you know that?"

"From doing crossword puzzles," Mom said.

Mom and I parked outside the square and walked fast to keep warm. "The students have all gone home for the holidays," Mom said. "Where should we start?"

I pointed to the first bookstore we passed. Mom went upstairs to the Art–Cooking–Travel–Calendar section. I tried Fantasy but nothing seemed right. I looked in Science Fiction, too, but I wasn't sure what Gus had already read. The covers looked alike: dragons and wizards, or spacecrafts and aliens. When Mom came downstairs, I still hadn't made any choices.

"Let's look at posters," she said.

We went across the street to the Coop. The posters were on the second floor and I saw it as soon as I walked up the stairs, Albert Einstein sticking out his tongue. Underneath the picture was his quote: *Imagination is more important than knowledge.* Mom helped me pick out the right size frame for it, and the salesgirl mounted it while we waited.

"I want to look in the Crafts Collective and then let's have lunch at the Garden House. They might have a fire going in the little dining room," Mom said.

We got a table in a window alcove. I could see the fire burning in the fireplace, and the little garden outside, too. While we were reading the menu, the snow started.

"Look, Mom," I said. "Snow!"

"A fire burning and good things to eat, and we can relax and watch the snow fall. Isn't this perfect?"

I nodded. It felt cozy and calm, the two of us ordering lunch, watching the snow, no rush, nowhere we had to get to.

"I like Christmas," I said.

"I hate it," Mom said. "Not right now, but usually. It's so frantic. I get nutty trying to find the perfect presents."

"Like the poster for Gus."

"See? We all try to find the right thing and then we worry that it isn't right at all, and maybe people won't know we love them, or they won't love us back. Or maybe someone unexpected will spring a present on us and we won't have one for them. It's crazy."

I looked out at the snow. It had already covered the

sidewalk and the flakes were coming down hard and thick. Someone had put a red mitten on a prong of the wrought-iron fence, hoping the owner might claim it.

The waitress came and we ordered minestrone, the soup of the day. I asked for a corn muffin and Mom picked a croissant.

"We'll choose dessert later," Mom said to the waitress.

Steam rose off the soup when the waitress set the bowls on the table. I stirred it, letting up new curls. Music played softly from a record or a radio—flutes, bells, and a drum—music people might have danced to in a castle five hundred years ago.

"We haven't talked much about what happened to you," Mom said.

I stirred my soup some more.

"I wish I had some brilliant advice that would make everything make sense again. That's what I'm supposed to do, right? If this were 'The Brady Bunch?' " Mom laughed at herself. "We have to talk about it. Otherwise," she paused and smoothed the wrinkle between her eyebrows, "we're pretending nothing happened. But it did happen and it could have been much worse, we both know that. That's why we have to talk. I don't want you to bury this inside, and let it hide there like some old, secret fear."

She looked out the window for a minute. Wood in the fireplace popped and the logs resettled.

"What happened to you proves we live in a scary world. I hate that. I even thought about moving to the country. Joining a firm in Vermont. Getting us away from Boston.

Away from the violence. We wouldn't have to be so careful or frightened. What do you think?"

"Move away from our house?"

She nodded.

"Do we have to?"

"No, we don't have to. I want to know what you think. Are you afraid here?"

"A little," I admitted. "But it's getting better. It's like that summer at the beach when the undertow caught me and I couldn't get to shore. You had to come and pull me in."

"I remember. You were about eight. That was scary!"

"I wouldn't go in over my knees for the rest of the summer. But the next year, I started swimming again. I'm more careful, though. Maybe that's what will happen. I'll stop feeling scared but I'll be careful."

Mom listened, frowning in concentration. "I don't like the idea of living in a place where you're scared. The whole thing reminds me of Emma. Men can't be trusted—all that crap she told you."

I laughed. Mom almost never swore. "I didn't believe Emma," I said. That was true. I didn't believe her. But I did feel uneasy about men since the attack. Even Gus. I didn't know how to explain that.

As if my thoughts were words, Mom said, "Do you feel differently about men now, after what happened?"

I nodded, embarrassed. I wasn't comfortable talking about this with my mother.

"See, that's what we have to talk about. I don't want

you to generalize from one experience." She sighed. "Miranda, this is hard. You're going to have to take my word for a lot. Maybe if your father was alive, we could have explained it better together. But I'll do my best."

The waitress cleared her throat, and picked up our soup bowls. "Care for some dessert?"

"Tea and pastry?" Mom asked. I nodded, so she told the waitress, "Two teas with milk and would you bring the pastry tray over?"

We watched her balance the big tray as she walked between the tables. I chose an éclair and Mom picked hazelnut torte.

We ate a few bites. Then Mom started again. "What I want you to believe is that sex is nothing to be afraid of. What almost happened with that man in the hall wasn't about sex. It was about violence, and power, and anger. Sex can be used that way, as a means of proving that you can hurt someone, and forcing them because you're stronger. But that's not normal."

I stared out the window. The snow had covered the mitten, turning it into a white lump on the fence post.

"With a man who cares about you, someone you love, someone who loves you, sex is about caring and knowing each other. It should never be about power and force. Do you believe me?"

I nodded.

"Good. I'm not saying that sex is something to take lightly. It's nothing to rush into, ever. But when you're old enough, and sure about what you're doing, when you know each other well, and you're with someone you love and trust, it's as close as you can get. It's just the opposite of what could have happened in the hall—just the opposite."

She looked at me hard, as if trying to see if her words had gone inside my mind. I traced the scallops on the edge of my place mat. "That's a lot to take in. Any questions?"

I shook my head, relieved the conversation was over.

"I think that's enough for now." She reached over and held my hand. "If I could make it so the attack never happened, I would. You know that, don't you, sweetheart?"

I smiled and she smiled. "You're such a good kid," she said.

We finished our tea, and wrapped up against the snow. By the time we reached the car, our coats were white. We had to scrape snow off the windshield with our mittens because the scraper was in the trunk and the lock had frozen. Mom drove home slowly. The soup and tea were warm inside me and so was the memory of her words in my mind as we sat in our little car, just the two of us, surrounded by a cloud of blowing snow. I slipped my hand under her arm and gave it a squeeze.

That evening when it was time to go caroling, the snow was still falling, but gently, and the wind had stopped. Gus knocked on the door.

"Come upstairs when you're ready and pick out a lantern. Mom made them out of tin cans," he said.

Last year when we went caroling, I froze. This time I put on long underwear, two pairs of socks, a turtleneck, a wool shirt, a sweater, jeans, ski pants, boots, my parka, a hat and scarf, and down mittens. I waddled upstairs to Gus's. Even Sebastian in his snowsuit wasn't as padded as I was.

Carol had decorated tin cans by hammering nail holes in them. When the candles inside were lit, the designs glowed. Mine had a row of fir trees. I picked out one for Mom with spirals all over it. In the front hall, Matt lit the candles, and we went down to the sidewalk. We walked toward the little park at the end of the street where Mr. Anthony was giving out the song booklets as he did every year. Some people had flashlights, but we had the only lanterns.

"We'll open with 'O Come All Ye Faithful,' page seven," Mr. Anthony said. "We proceed down Warren, then Brookline, then Canton. It's too cold, definitely too cold to plan any further. Does everyone agree?"

My mother giggled. She always said Mr. Anthony should've stayed in the army, he liked to order people around so much.

At the first house, Sebastian rang the doorbell. When we came to the lines, "Oh, come let us adore him," Mr. Anthony motioned for us to sing softly the first time, then louder and louder. At the end of the song, the people inside offered us shortbread from a red tin.

We sang "Here we come a-wassailing" as we walked down the block. At the next house people crowded to look out the front windows. We sang "O Little Town of Bethlehem" and "Joy to the World." They gave us red and white striped ribbon candy.

As we crossed the street I slipped on an icy patch. Gus

grabbed my arm to keep me from falling, and I didn't pull away. He kept hold of my arm and we stood close together in the cold, sharing a songbook after that. As we sang, I remembered walking home Halloween night, close together, and dancing together at the Thanksgiving dance. It wasn't awkward then, and it wasn't now. We stood side by side in our down jackets, arm in padded arm. Gus was my first friend—he'd always been my friend. What happened in the hall with a strange man didn't change that. It didn't have anything to do with it.

18

The Llewellyns left on Christmas Eve for their Aunt Rita's house in Vermont. With them away and Tina at her parents', the house was quiet. We decorated the tree and had oyster stew for supper like we always do, this time with Angie and Richard, friends of Mom's from work. After dessert, we played charades with phrases like "jingle bells" and "Santa's sleigh."

After Angie and Richard said merry Christmas and went home, Mom and I turned off the lights and sat in the living room admiring the tree. Little white lights made the ornaments and the tinsel shine. Outside, new snow gleamed on the trees and roofs. The night looked magical, not at all scary.

On Christmas morning, we opened our presents, taking turns. The Llewellyns and Tina had left gifts, and a package from Emma had come, too, so when we added our own, there was a pile under the bottom branches.

The first present Mom opened was from Carol—a deep purple blouse, a good match for the scarf I'd chosen.

I opened a box from Catherine next. The card said, *You are too old enough. Love, Catherine.* Inside was a silky peach camisole and matching underpants, edged with white lace, nothing like my cotton underpants.

Mom whistled. "What a sweet present. Why didn't I think of that?"

"I'm going to wear them today when we go to Aunt Lucia's." We were driving up around noon.

Next, Mom opened my scarf box. "Irises! My favorite." She tried it against the blouse. "Look how pretty they are together. I'll wear them today. You in your peach lingerie and me in my purple. We'll be glamorous."

I opened presents from Emma, Sebastian, Carol, and Matt: a watch, pencils, and an Irish cable-knit sweater. Mom gave me clothes, too. She also gave me two books, a poetry collection and a thin book with a blue cloth cover—the letters on the cover were stamped in gold: *The Tempest* by William Shakespeare. Inside, she'd written, "Meet your namesake, Miranda."

"My namesake?"

Mom nodded. "Your father and I named you after Shakespeare's Miranda. We hoped you'd have her sense of

166

wonder. Miranda grows up on an enchanted island far away from society. She finally meets humans when she's a young woman. Listen to what she says. 'How beauteous mankind is! O brave new world that has such people in't!' "

Mom smiled at me. "We hoped you'd feel that way, too."

She handed me the book and I read the lines myself as she watched me. "My namesake. I like that. I'll read the whole thing," I said.

The last present I opened was from Gus. It was a new notebook, a felt-tip pen, a sweatshirt covered with the names of famous writers—Dickens, Twain, Frost, and a hundred more—and a folder with a chapter from *Alien Attraction* entitled "Vortrum's Farewell."

What was he talking about? He couldn't make Vortrum go away. We hadn't even talked about it. I put the folder aside until we finished with the presents.

When we'd both opened everything, we made a fire from all the wadded-up wrapping paper and Mom went in to change for Aunt Lucia's. I sat in the rocker and read Gus's chapter.

"Vortrum's Farewell," he'd titled it. It was a letter.

Dear Teresa,

 I have packed my flight bag and contacted my ship. This letter is all I have left to do before departing from your planet. I know that it would be more manly of me to tell you myself, but I cannot. I am not manly. I am not human. That is the trouble, I think.

 Ever since we went for our sleigh ride the day of

the big snow, when I thought we were under enemy attack and you taught me a lesson in meteorology, you have been unfriendly to me. Before, you were my closest human friend. You showed me how to eat the hot dog and roll, and how to wind the spaghetti around the fork. You taught me to say the correct expressions: hi, see you, okay. Without you I would never have understood the game of football or the dance at the gym. At home, only the sea snakes wiggle the way you showed me at the dance.

I thought we were true friends, Teresa. At home, when someone gives you a bracelet woven from the trust vine, you are pledged friends for life. I gave you my bracelet after the dance.

On the day of the snow when you took me on the sled and we went together down the long hill at the golf course, you steered and I held onto your waist. What happened to our friendship that day? Was it because my skin turned green from the snow? The chemical that seals my inner layers from the cold turns my skin in the same process. Perhaps it was the kiss we made when the toboggan tipped over beside the pine tree. Kissing is not a custom on my planet but I found it pleasurable. My skin faded quickly from green, did you notice?

Since the sledding, you have been unfriendly, Teresa. You say, "No, thanks," when I suggest a plan. You never sit beside me in class any more, or in the cafeteria. You walk with girls and leave me behind, alone.

My research assignment is completed and there is no reason for me to stay now. I am lonely. Good-bye, Teresa. I never pretended to be human, although perhaps my disguise misled you. I hoped it would not matter. I thought we could be friends even if we were different. Thank you for the many ways you helped me. I will always think of you when I think of Earth.

    I remain your friend from Interstixus,
    Vortrum

Gus had drawn a picture of Vortrum, with green skin, on the toboggan with Teresa. Another drawing showed Vortrum signaling to his ship, standing by himself in his backyard holding something like a garlic press in his hand. Gus didn't show them kissing. I would have. That was the best part.

As we drove to Aunt Lucia's I thought about Gus's chapter. I hoped he'd written it before the caroling. He was right, I had been unfriendly, especially after the day we went skating. But it wasn't as if I'd stopped being friends. It was just awkward for a while.

For Christmas dinner we had goose, just like in the play. Uncle Davis and Ray had picked out a tree as round as it was tall. It filled the whole bay in the living room, and the house smelled of pine.

Being the youngest, I got to blow out the candles after dinner, and make a wish on each. I made the same wish twice, about Gus and me. Tina drove back to the city with us, her presents crammed into a shopping bag. When we got home it was too late to stay up and write, but the next morning, I got up early and wrote at the kitchen table while Mom and Tina were still sleeping. I wore my new sweatshirt and used my new felt-tip. My *Alien Attraction* notebook was half full.

First I drew a picture of Teresa reading Vortrum's letter, just to warm up. It had been weeks since I'd written. Then I started.

> Teresa read the letter that she found under the mail slot. She grabbed her coat and ran to Vortrum's house. As she ran, she watched the sky in case a spaceship appeared. She found Vortrum sitting on the steps in back of his house. "Thank goodness you're still here," she said. "I was afraid you'd be gone."
>
> Vortrum nodded. "I hoped my ship would come quickly."
>
> "I wish you wouldn't go," Teresa said.
>
> "I have made my decision."
>
> "Can't you change your mind? Tell the ship not to land. I'm sorry I've been acting mean. It's not because you're different. But the kiss made me shy," Teresa said.
>
> "I have sent the message to my ship. I cannot stay," Vortrum said.

I stopped there and chewed on the end of my pen, not sure what to say next. Should I make them kiss? What could I do about the spaceship? I wished I was as good a writer as Gus.

"*To be continued,*" I wrote at the end. Gus could write

the end of the chapter with me. He was the one to decide if Vortrum would change his mind and stay.

What could Teresa do to convince Vortrum?

I drew four lines through "*To be continued,*" and started writing again.

> *Teresa sat down beside Vortrum on the steps and held his hand. It was a little green but the color faded as she held it.*
>
> *"Vortrum, I don't want you to go. Why not stay until summer? You've never seen spring, you've never gone swimming."*
>
> *Before Vortrum could answer, she leaned over and kissed him.*

Then I wrote, "*To be continued,*" again. That would give Gus plenty to work on. I wondered if he'd be surprised by the kiss. Maybe not. The kiss on the toboggan was his idea.

I didn't want to rip the pages out of my notebook, so I wrapped the whole thing up in red shiny Christmas paper that I found in the hall closet. After breakfast, I'd give it to Gus and ask if he wanted to work on the story later. I'd missed him, missed sitting on the window seat with him. I missed his laugh, and his long green sneakers dangling off the edge of the cushion. I'd say, "Want to work on *Alien Attraction* with me?" And he'd say "Sure." When you've been friends as long as we had, you know what to expect.